Jericho's Child

A Cozy Regency Romance

Jolie Beaumont

ASTER PRESS

First published 2014

Published and distributed by:
Aster Press
Kansas-Jerusalem
asterpressbooks@gmail.com

CHAPTER I

SOPHIE MOORE GLANCED OUT THE window of the carriage, which had come to a halt before a fine-looking Mayfair residence. *Too fine*, she thought, *for someone like me*. Her worries only increased when a servant clad in smart livery opened the front door and marched down the spotless front steps.

"Courage, Sophie, dear," said her companion, Mrs. Hemingway, giving the girl's arm a reassuring pat. "It may not be what you are used to, but soon it will feel like home. Isn't that so, Mr. Hemingway?"

The matronly woman's husband nodded his head vigorously. "Quite so. Quite so. I am sure your late father's friends are fine people. Nothing to worry about there, I am sure."

Mr. Hemingway might have gone on, for it was his habit to repeat himself when he found himself to be in a socially awkward situation. In Jamaica, the island from which the small party had recently come, he had been in charge of a British garrison's horses, and in truth he was much more comfortable when in the presence of four-legged creatures than ladies. Thankfully, at least in his opinion, he did not need to say more, since the servant had arrived and was already opening the carriage door and letting down the steps.

Sophie eyed the servant with much less equanimity. However, there was nothing to do but say goodbye to the only real friends she had had in the seventeen years she had lived in this world — friends who had known her father and served as her companions and guardians while she grew up in her father's garrison, a lonely child and one who had been orphaned of her mother at birth.

"You will write?" asked Sophie, still not wanting to part.

"As soon as we are settled at my sister's place in Kent," replied Mrs. Hemingway. "We shall both have much to tell. Now, put a smile on your face, for your father's sake. That is how he always faced the world. Isn't that so, Mr. Hemingway?"

"Quite so, Mrs. Hemingway. Quite so."

Encouraged by her friends' words, Sophie forced her lips to turn upward and then she turned away from the familiar faces of the smiling couple. No matter what lay behind that imposing Mayfair door, she would not let her fears cast aspersion upon her late father and the upbringing he had given her, she decided. Even when she heard the carriage drive away behind her, she kept her eyes firmly upon the path that lay before her, uncertain though it was.

The servant wordlessly showed her into a drawing room. Although she was no expert, she knew it was furnished with the best that money could buy. All was gleaming wood and plush Turkey carpets and elegant brocade. While she was wondering if people really dared to sit on such graceful settees and chairs, she realized there was indeed a person who dared — and this person was stonily examining her through a quizzing glass.

"Do not stand there in the doorway, Miss Moore. You are letting in all the cold air. Come here." The woman pointed to a seat by the fire, whose pleasantly glowing flames looked inviting, even if the woman's bony finger did not.

"Thank you, ma'am," said Sophie as she took the offered seat. It was only when she felt the warmth of the fire upon her face that she realized how cold and tired she was.

"Sir Charles sends his compliments and his regrets," the woman continued. "He has been detained in Parliament. You will meet him at dinner tonight at six o'clock and be on time. Sir Charles is very particular about his dinner being served precisely at six."

"Yes, ma'am." The mention of dinner made Sophie realize she was famished as well, and she wondered if there would be a nuncheon before then. If not, she would have to make friends with one of the servants at once, someone who could beg a plate of cold meat from the cook.

"I am not altogether displeased by this opportunity to speak with you alone, Miss Moore." A thin smile played upon the woman's lips, but it did nothing to improve her faded, angular looks. Neither did her dress. Although made from fashionable white sprigged muslin, the snowy color only emphasized the sad fact that the woman had not been in the first blush of youth for many, many dreary English winters.

"As the sister of Sir Charles, and the person responsible for the smooth running of his household since the death of his wife five years ago," Miss Wentworth continued, "it is my duty to speak frankly, so there will be no misunderstandings. My brother has a kind heart, which is why you have been invited to stay here, until your future is decided. But that kindness does not extend to your marrying either of his two sons. I do not expect you to be so foolish as to set your cap at Mr. Wentworth, who will inherit the title and estate. But even Henry Wentworth is not for you, Miss Moore. Please to remember that during your stay."

Having said her piece, Miss Dorothea Wentworth, for that was the woman's name, rose from her seat and pulled upon a silken embroidered cord fitted with a tassel on the end.

"A nuncheon will be waiting for you in the blue sitting room, after you freshen up." Miss Wentworth raised her quizzing glass to her eye a second time. "I hope you have brought warm clothes with you, Miss Moore. We have had an exceptionally cold winter, and the spring promises to be the same."

A moment later, a servant soundlessly entered.

"Show Miss Moore to her room."

Sophie followed the servant back to the entranceway, where a draft made her shiver. She could very well believe that she was in for a cold season.

CHAPTER II

EVEN THE THOUGHT OF THE waiting food did nothing to raise Sophie's depressed spirits. Neither did the sight of the bedroom, which was comfortably, if not luxuriously appointed. She mechanically splashed some of the warm water from the porcelain ewer into the accompanying basin and washed the dust of the journey from her face and hands. Meanwhile, the maid was extracting her few dresses and other belongings from her small trunk and bandbox, placing the garments inside the commodious wardrobe that sat against one of the walls. Sophie's set of mirror, comb and hairbrush — backed with matching mother of pearl, and one of Sophie's few really fine possessions — were placed on the dressing table.

The maid was momentarily stumped, though, when she came to the bottom of the trunk and pulled out a thick sheaf of music, the pages neatly tied together with a ribbon. Looking about the room for an appropriate place to set the pages, her eye fell upon a library couch, which had been placed at the foot of the bed, and said, "Shall I place your music here, miss?"

Sophie regarded the long and narrow library couch, which had been fashioned in the Egyptian style and covered with a pale blue fabric that matched the room's curtains, and wondered why one person would need two beds to sleep upon. She had much to learn about London practices and habits, she supposed.

Sophie also supposed she should exchange her traveling costume for something less tousled, before going downstairs, but a spirit of rebellion was starting to make itself felt in her heart. *Set my cap at her nephews*, she grumbled as she brushed out her tangled curls. *As though I would be interested in marrying a London tulip!* She jabbed a hair pin into a mess of curls. *I am sure I shan't speak more than two words to either one of them for the duration of ...*

She stopped with her brush in midair. She had no idea how long her host intended her visit to last, no idea what she would do when Sir Charles decided her visit had come to an end. It was not as if Sir Charles was a relative and she had any real claim upon him. Of course, she had heard the famous story dozens of times, how her father had saved the life of Sir Charles on the battlefield. It had happened during the revolt of the American Colonies, at a place called Guilford Court House, in the southern part of what would become the United States of America. The British had won the battle, which lasted little more than an hour. But the fighting had been fierce and many brave soldiers and officers lost their lives or were wounded.

Sir Charles had been one of the wounded. In the chaos after the battle, he and her father, who had been just a lad of fourteen at the time, had gotten separated from the rest of the regiment and spent a stormy night in the forest. Her father had given his coat to Sir Charles, to shelter the feverish officer from the pouring rain, and given all that was left of his meager rations as well. Thus, Sir Charles survived that miserable night and in the morning some British soldiers found the half-dead pair and brought them to shelter.

After the war, Sir Charles returned to England, to resume his life as a gentleman, while her father had remained in the army, joining a regiment in Jamaica. But every year at Christmas, her father received a package of delicious food accompanied by a note from Sir Charles, where that gentleman reiterated his thanks and his wish to be of service to her father, so he could repay the favor. Her father had sent his thanks, but the favor he stored up for a future date — which occurred the previous spring, when he realized he would not live out the year.

Sophie herself had written the letter to Sir Charles, since her father was already too weak to sit at the table for long periods of time. In it, she mentioned that she was musical — she played both the harp and the pianoforte — and so she hoped to establish herself either as private teacher of the musical arts or open a school, thereby making it clear she had no intention of being a permanent burden.

The letter was sent, and then came the long, anxious wait for a reply. How many hours had she sat by her father's bedside, trying to soothe his worries by inventing stories about the letter's supposed journey — humorous adventures to explain the letter's delay. Thankfully, the letter from Sir Charles arrived in time, with his offer to give Sophie a home until she would be able to find a position in England. A letter of credit for a generous sum of money to take care of her needs during the long voyage to England was also included. Her father had therefore died in peace, knowing he had done all he could to provide for his only child.

"Pardon me for saying so, miss, but you will feel better when you have some food inside you."

Sophie looked up and into the mirror. In the reflection she saw the maid standing behind her and gazing at her with a warm smile. She also saw that tears were streaming down her own face. Sophie quickly wiped away the tears and smiled back, grateful for the first kind words she had received since stepping over the threshold of the house.

"Thank you ..."

"Joan, miss. Shall I show you the way to the blue sitting room?"

"Yes, I am hungry. Thank you, Joan."

There was no one in the blue sitting room when Sophie entered. But at the end of the room, which true to its name was decorated in calming shades of pale blue, accented by streaks and flecks of rich golden colored thread, platters of cold meat and fruit and cake had been set upon a mahogany buffet.

Sophie heaped her plate high. Growing up among soldiers, who always had a healthy appetite, she had never felt ashamed to eat a hearty meal, even when among company. The urn had also been prepared, and so she helped herself to a steaming cup of tea.

As she settled into a seat, she decided to banish all distressing thoughts for the duration of the meal and give her full attention to each welcome bite. Yet, no sooner had she began her culinary devotions than her attention was distracted by an object that fell into her teacup with a splash that made some of the tea spill onto the saucer. She fished out the object with her silver spoon and examined the prize — a small lump of sugar!

She looked around the room, curious to see who had thrown the sugar into her tea, but there was no one there but herself. Perhaps another young lady would have been disturbed by the incident, but Sophie had not grown up on an island for nothing. Strange people passed through Jamaica, each with a tale and a quirk. There was old One-Eyed Armstrong, whom some folks said had been a pirate in his younger days, thanks to the parrot he kept, the patch over his left eye and his impressive knowledge of winds and tides. The parrot, Tripoli, had been known to remove things from the serving bowls and deposit them on people's plates, usually with an impolite comment. Then there was Jimmy Spindle, who had been all over the world (or so he said) and kept a small monkey on his shoulder at all times. The monkey would pick fruit off the trees and hurl it at people it didn't like, which was half the island most of the time. Sophie therefore assumed that Sir Charles must have some pet which had gotten loose and was amusing itself by throwing lumps of sugar into her tea. For already another lump had joined the first.

Sophie solved the problem in her own way, by removing her plate of food to another part of the room. But when a lump of sugar landed on her head while she was making a fresh cup of tea, she decided that enough was enough. Taking up the poker that sat next to the fireplace, she aimed it up at the ceiling, certain the animal must have some secret hiding place above the paneled surface, where there was some small hole through which it could look down. Much to her surprise, her first poke met with success for she was greeted with a howl — yet one that sounded suspiciously human.

"Who is up there?" she demanded. "Reveal yourself at once, or I shall shoot you with my pistol."

A few seconds later, she heard a thud, not overhead but to the right of the fireplace. Then a section of the paneled wall swung open and a young man entered the room, with his hands raised above his head.

"I shouldn't shoot, if I were you," said the young man. "I am only the younger son, it is true, but Aunt Dorothea would not like the mess."

Sophie lowered the poker, and a blush began to rise from her throat to her cheeks. "Beg your pardon, sir," she said, giving a quick curtsy. "I thought you were a monkey."

"And I beg your pardon for disappointing you," replied Henry Wentworth. "May I lower my hands now?"

"Of course!" Sophie's cheeks burned red even more fiercely.

"Do you really have a pistol with you?"

"No, I only said it to frighten you."

"You certainly succeeded."

"Well, you should not have thrown sugar lumps into my tea." She was about to add that his behavior was more suited to a boy still in the nursery than a gentleman who from his appearance seemed to be at least twenty. But in the nick of time she recalled that he was a member of the family and she was not, and therefore it was not her place to rebuke him.

"I only wished to see who you were, when you are not on your best behavior, which I assume you will be at dinner," said Henry.

"And who am I?" asked Sophie, warming to the young man, despite his strange manners.

"Courageous, independent, quick-thinking, a young lady of spirit — all of which I must tell you is totally useless, perhaps even a great handicap, in London society."

"Are London ladies insipid, then?"

"Yes."

Henry Wentworth gave her a smile. Sophie smiled back. Although the younger son was not good-looking by classical standards, there was something very likeable about his perfectly ordinary features. Brown hair, a healthy complexion, average height and build, pale blue eyes, a slightly lopsided nose — as though his Maker had been called away in the middle of fashioning it and never returned to finish the job — yes, there was something reassuringly English about Henry Wentworth.

"Do you mind if I join you? I am famished," he continued. "I am supposed to be at my club and eating my beefsteak there."

"Are you not afraid Miss Wentworth will enter and see us together?"

"Frankly, no. I know I must marry money. I like the comforts of life too much to give them up for a young lady with a pretty face and a charming way with a poker."

Henry filled a plate and beckoned for Sophie to retake her place at the table. Soon they were seated companionably, enjoying their meal and the company.

"Do you and your brother often spy on people?" asked Sophie, glancing up at the ceiling.

"I used to quite a bit, when I was young. But Arthur, that is my older brother, never stooped to such childish games. I believe he has been a nonpareil from the cradle."

"He is one of those rare specimens of the human race that are perfect in every way?"

"Yes, I am afraid he is."

"It must be very boring for him, and you."

"I cannot speak for Arthur, and in truth I do not think he objects to be universally admired. But, yes, for me it is a bit of bore. Of course, it has its positive aspect as well. No one expects much of me, just as no one expects the moon to outshine the sun."

"I suppose I shall not like Mr. Wentworth very much," said Sophie, visualizing a cold and haughty Corinthian in her mind, the type that figured in some of the novels she had read in Jamaica. The depictions in those novels, left behind by occasional female visitors to the island, were all she really knew about England.

Henry silently regarded the pretty young woman sitting across from him, whose gaze had already left him for some other faraway and dreamy point. "On the contrary, you shall fall in love with him. Every woman does."

CHAPTER III

SOPHIE SAT HUNCHED OVER HER jewelry box, trying to decide whether she should wear the necklace with the garnets, which had belonged to her mother, or the cameo necklace that had been a gift from her father on the occasion of her seventeenth birthday—the last one they had shared together. Then she angrily snapped the box shut and reached for a colored ribbon instead. Joan, who had been trying to do Sophie's hair, glanced up at the unexpected noise. But Sophie did not care. She had caught herself in the act of trying to decide which necklace would most please and impress the resident nonpareil, and she was not about to let herself knowingly fall into that trap.

When she entered the drawing room at five minutes before the hour of six, the others were already assembled there.

"It is just us tonight, Miss Moore," said Sir Charles, after clasping her hand warmly and leading her further into the room and closer to the family circle. "I hope you will not be bored, but we thought you might want a quiet dinner your first night in London, after your long journey. You have already met my sister, Miss Wentworth, I understand."

Dorothea Wentworth gave Sophie a sour smile, which made Sophie wonder how two siblings could be so unalike. But she was grateful they were. She decided at once that she liked Sir Charles, who had a kind face and easy manners. Although his brown hair was liberally streaked with gray and he was tending toward stoutness, she could see an agreeable likeness between the patriarch of the family and Henry, the younger son.

Naturally, she could only steal a glance over at Henry Wentworth, since they were not yet supposed to have met. But she knew he was observing her carefully when Sir Charles turned to the elegant young man standing by the fireplace and said, "Arthur, come meet our visitor from Jamaica."

Mr. Wentworth strode to his father's side with the assurance that a fabulous fortune gives. For as Sophie and all the world knew, the Wentworth title was not exceptional, since it was only a baronetcy, but the Wentworth family was rich in land and had an income a Viscount (some said even an Earl) might envy. Therefore, Mr. Arthur Wentworth could greet the world on his own terms, certain those terms would be accepted by the *ton*, which was all the world that mattered to him, his family, and friends.

After a few polite enquiries about her journey, Arthur Wentworth nodded to his younger brother and Henry Wentworth came forward to be introduced. He and Sophie played their parts gallantly. Then they all went into dinner.

Because the party was so intimate, Sophie could naturally find occasions to observe the nonpareil. To her great disappointment, she saw that Arthur Wentworth was indeed a man worth noticing. She supposed he took after his deceased mother, since he did not look like anyone else in the room. His hair was dark, with silky curls that spilled down onto his forehead, almost touching the dark eyebrows that stood over eyes that were a brilliant sapphire blue.

His lips were full and even, neither curved up into a natural smile, nor curved downward in perpetual frown. In between was his strong, straight nose, which gave masculinity to a face that otherwise might be considered too pretty.

His figure was elegant, as were his clothes. In manners he was also everything a gentleman should be. He attended upon his aunt, making sure she received a good cut of meat and the freshest vegetables. He listened attentively to his father's stories about his army days — the days in the former American Colonies — and made appropriate expressions of surprise and interest, when such comments were called for. He also deigned to notice Miss Moore on a few occasions, signaling to a servant to fill the young lady's empty wine glass, inquiring whether she found the béchamel sauce to her taste or preferred another.

And yet ...

Sophie could not quite put her finger upon what was wrong, what marred the otherwise perfect picture. She had the sense she was watching a play, one where the leading actor was faultless and yet not entirely present. She could well believe that Arthur Wentworth was bored, having only his immediate family and herself to entertain him. Yet, she felt she could also sense a deeper emptiness — the emptiness of a young man who has had everything good in the world handed to him upon a silver platter, without his having had to make the slightest effort to earn a single thing.

Or perhaps that was only the romantic in her speaking. Perhaps she wanted Arthur Wentworth to be more than the perfect English gentleman, because ...

She saw Henry looking at her and smiling. He had caught her in the act. She was falling in love with Arthur Wentworth—but, it was not really love, she assured herself. She was just overtired, which was why she was letting her imagination momentarily run wild.

After the meal, Sophie retired to her room. She knew from the dinner conversation that Henry was going to the theatre that evening, while Arthur Wentworth was continuing on to a ball. She supposed, as she slipped into her nightgown and nestled under the covers, that Mr. Wentworth would be surrounded by a bevy of dazzling beauties, each one vying for his attention. And she could see him, in her half-dream state, taking his place in the line of dancers, reaching out his hand to his partner ...

And since this was her dream, that partner was her.

THE NEXT FEW DAYS PASSED quietly. To Sophie's great relief, extreme vexation and every emotion in between, the only time she saw Mr. Wentworth was in her dreams. It seemed that the sought after young man had a full schedule every day: early morning rides in the park, followed by breakfast invitations, excursions to see the new pictures in the galleries or the horses at Tattersall's, morning calls, afternoon teas, supper invitations, then off to the theatre or the opera or a gaming hell or a small or large ball.

Henry Wentworth was also away most of the day and night, but he always found a few moments to ask

Sophie about her health or share a funny story he had heard or offer to be of service in some way.

Since she had no one except Miss Wentworth to converse with, and that was a pleasure neither lady wished to overindulge in, Sophie spent most of the first day of her visit in her room, writing a long letter to Mrs. Hemingway, assuring the older woman that she was safe and becoming accustomed to her new surroundings.

The second day found her in the library, a well-stocked room that reflected the wide tastes of several generations of Wentworths. Although she found the doric columns and the occasional Roman bust peering down at her from atop a bookcase to be ridiculously grand, the wing back chairs placed before the fireplace looked comfortable, and she could imagine herself spending many a pleasant hour lost in a good novel or travel album.

Sir Charles had also instructed the servants to bring down the harp from the attic, where it had been stored after his wife had passed away, since no one else in the family played it, and in the afternoon a place was found for the harp in the blue sitting room. Miss Wentworth grimly informed Sophie that the room was infrequently used, since the gentlemen of the family were so often away from home, and therefore Sophie could play the harp whenever she pleased, undisturbed.

The thought of playing the harp undisturbed did not please Sophie as much as it should have, since by nature she enjoyed company and was beginning to find tedious the long hours she was spending alone. She therefore eagerly accepted Sir Charles's suggestion that she should play for the family after dinner that evening.

After she tuned the harp, which had not fared too badly during its sojourn in the attic, she spent the rest of the afternoon leafing through the pages of her music. As she considered each piece — its technical requirements, its length, its ability to please a range of listeners — she openly acknowledged her dual objectives for the evening.

Of course, she wished to impress the family with her playing so they would see she was, indeed, a talented musician and had the skills to make an excellent teacher. The second reason made Sophie smile. She assumed Arthur Wentworth was not purposely ignoring her; there was no reason why he should feel compelled to so do. On the other hand, he had made no effort to acknowledge her presence in the house after that first evening, which seemed to suggest he simply did not find her worthy of his notice. Here therefore was an opportunity to force Mr. Wentworth to take notice of her and adjust his opinion. For if she could not meet Mr. Arthur Wentworth as an equal in terms of fortune and title, she could certainly show him she was the equal of his female acquaintances in terms of intelligence, taste and accomplishments. Yes, she would show him he had been wrong to ignore her so completely, if only as a point of honor.

However, her efforts to create a pleasing musical evening turned out to have been in vain. Once again, only Sir Charles and Miss Wentworth were present at dinner, since the two young gentlemen had other engagements, which they could not bow out of.

"Even a younger son has his uses on the dance floor, if only to make the numbers even between the gentlemen and the ladies," Henry had told her, when making his apologies. Yet, there was something about his manner that told Sophie the young man did not entirely regret having to forgo her concert to attend a private ball. She supposed there was some young lady who had won his heart, and he expected to see her there.

Despite the scanty attendance, Sophie played well at her "concert." She could tell that neither Sir Charles nor Miss Wentworth was particularly musical. After a busy day in Parliament and at his club, Sir Charles found it difficult to keep open his drooping eyes. Miss Wentworth was wide awake, but very busy with some embroidery work that apparently required her full attention. Although Sir Charles did compliment Sophie profusely after she was finished playing, Sophie went up to bed feeling slightly depressed.

By the third day of being cooped inside with only Miss Wentworth as a companion during the day, Sophie felt she might go mad. She was therefore very grateful to hear she would have a visitor the next day, Lady Harrington, the niece of Sir Charles's late wife, who had added luster and lucre to the family when she married a Viscount seven months previously.

Sir Charles had promised that Sophie would like the Viscountess — "Not at all high in the instep, even though she is now a grand lady," he had assured her — and he had not been mistaken. Lady Harrington had the same dark hair, pleasing features and graceful carriage as her cousin, Mr. Wentworth. But unlike her cousin, underneath her perfect manners was a warmth and gaiety that immediately brightened a previously dull morning.

Sophie, Sir Charles and Miss Wentworth were in the drawing room when Lady Harrington called. After the introductions and initial enquiries had been concluded, Lady Harrington turned to Sophie and said, "First, we must go shopping, Miss Moore. This cold spell in March has taken all of us by surprise. But for you, who have grown up in warmer climes, the cold must be unbearable."

Sophie was charmed by the idea and was about to say so, when Miss Wentworth said, "Should we not first decide Miss Moore's future? London frippery will be of no use to her if she will be taking a position as governess in April or May."

The word "governess" immediately cast a pall upon the gathering, like a cold blast of air that reminds those near the fire there is an unpleasant storm raging outside. However, Lady Harrington dispelled the gloom with her silvery-toned laugh. "Even a governess needs a warm shawl," she said, fingering her own shawl, which was a striking salmon-colored length of soft wool that ended in a wide paisley-patterned border of salmon and emerald green, and which she wore casually draped over her full-length, salmon-colored pelisse. Sophie imagined it would probably take a governess half a lifetime to earn enough money to be able to afford a shawl like that.

"And Miss Moore must have a new dress for the ball you are giving in honor of Henry's twenty-first birthday, Sir Charles." Before Miss Wentworth could object, Lady Harrington added, "Every young lady should have a new gown for her first London ball."

"You are right, Mary," Sir Charles said, beaming. Lady Harrington had always been a favorite of his, since he had not had daughters of his own to admire and indulge. "Take charge of Miss Moore. I am sure my dear wife would have done the same, if she were still with us."

"Is Miss Moore to be treated as a member of the family, then?" inquired Miss Wentworth, with a tone of voice fairly dripping with disdain.

"Well, we hardly need a governess here, Dorothea," replied Sir Charles, "unless you feel a need to brush up on your French or sums."

While Sir Charles laughed at his little joke, Lady Harrington deftly turned the conversation to a different topic. A few minutes later, the visitor went on her way. Sophie found an excuse to leave the room, which left Dorothea Wentworth alone with her brother.

"Really, Sir Charles," she began, emphasizing the word "Sir" as she often did when her brother vexed her, "you cannot mean to introduce that young pauper to society."

A frown settled upon Sir Charles's face. "In truth, I was not sure what to do. But I trust Mary's judgment. If she takes Miss Moore under her wing, society will follow."

"And what then? I think not only of our family's reputation, but what of the girl? How will she return to her proper place, after her head has been turned by a season of shopping and balls?"

"I know, we shall ask Miss Moore to play the harp. We will have a little musical interlude in between the dancing. That will explain her presence at the ball and serve to introduce her to society."

Although Sir Charles was very impressed by his cleverness, Miss Wentworth still was not appeased. When Arthur Wentworth entered the room, Dorothea turned to him for support. However, the young man did not seem overly concerned with the topic of Miss Moore.

"Besides, the ball for Henry's twenty-first birthday is sure to be a bore," he said. "This entire season has been nothing but a bore, so far. One cannot even go abroad, thanks to this interminable war."

"You might marry and settle down, if you are so bored," said Sir Charles. Although he enjoyed the reflected glory he received from having an heir who was universally admired, he did sometimes wish Arthur was not such an exquisite, both for the young man's sake and his own. In his long life, he had seen many a handsome young devil turned into a ridiculous, debauched roué in middle age, and he sincerely hoped that such would not be the fate of his eldest son.

"Young ladies do not wait forever, not even for London society's nonpareil," Sir Charles persisted. "Miss Bryce-Jones is a beauty, and she comes with a very handsome dowry—the best of the lot this season. Lady Jane Mortimer is the daughter of an Earl, and her family is one of the oldest in England. The estate in Somerset is not what it once was, I will admit, but there is a house in London and some property in Scotland that her father has promised to bestow upon the lucky man who wins her hand."

"And next season there will be another Miss Bryce-Jones and another Lady Jane, just as there were Miss Bryce-Joneses and Lady Janes the season before and the season before that. And with fashions being what they are and all the ladies wearing white, you cannot even tell the difference between them by their clothes."

"You are too young to be so jaded. What will you do when you are my age?"

Arthur shrugged and left the room.

"What on earth has gotten into him?" asked Miss Wentworth.

"Hopefully, it is just some chit of an actress who is playing hard to get and refusing to come to terms," replied Sir Charles, although he himself was not so sure this was the reason.

Miss Wentworth harrumphed, for she prided herself on maintaining old-fashioned morals in what was an unabashedly immoral era. At the same time, she resolved to keep a close eye on her nephew. A bored young man might fall prey to a novelty such as Miss Moore simply for the sake of having something out of the ordinary to do, and Miss Wentworth had her heart set on Arthur marrying Lady Jane. An Earl's daughter would add further luster to the family.

Arthur, however, was concerned neither with actresses nor daughters of Earls. He had an hour to spare before his boxing lesson and his one wish was to find an amusing way to fill it. That was not to say he was empty-headed, like some of the gentlemen in his set. Indeed, the tutors of his youth had generally complimented him upon his quick grasp of Latin and ability to intelligently discuss the writings of the ancients. But since his social duties as an adult did not require deep thinking, he had fallen into the habit of relying upon momentary sensations and mindless amusements to fill the long hours of the day. He was therefore on the way to the billiards room when he nearly barged into Sophie, who was coming out of the library with full speed, since she hoped to escape to her room with her book without being seen by Miss Wentworth.

"Beg your pardon, Miss Moore," he said with perfect politeness, since a lady could never be in the wrong. He stooped to pick up the book that had fallen from her hand. When he saw the book's cover he glanced at her with surprise, for it was a manual on fencing.

"You are interested in fencing, Miss Moore?"

"I used to watch my father and the other soldiers," Sophie replied, hoping her blushes were not noticeable.

"I thought that perhaps your father had taught you the art."

Sophie hesitated. In truth, her father had taught her. But it was one thing to show off her swordsmanship at a garrison in Jamaica, when she was still just a girl, and quite another to admit to such unladylike behavior in London, when she was already seventeen. Besides, she did not know Arthur Wentworth well enough to know whether his question was sincere or he was quizzing her. She therefore said, "My father always said a woman's tongue is sharper than the sword."

Mr. Wentworth returned the book to her hand, bowed and continued down the hall, to the billiards room, leaving Sophie to wonder whether she said the right thing or not—and very angry at herself for caring so much.

CHAPTER IV

LADY HARRINGTON ARRIVED THE NEXT day, full of plans and good spirits. She was in a difficult in between stage of her life — one where the excitement of her marriage and new station in society was beginning to wear off, but she did not yet have children to provide new interest — and so she was looking for some stimulating project. Sophie Moore, she decided, would do.

"We shall stop first at Clark and Debenham, for I cannot bear to see you shivering in that thin pelisse a moment longer," she informed Sophie. "They have some that are already made, and it will be easy to find one that suits you. With your complexion, I am certain you can wear most colors." She then added, casting an observant eye at Sophie's light pink pelisse, "I assume your six months of mourning are over?"

"Yes."

Sophie did not say more, since to her surprise the carriage had come to a halt on Cavendish Square. "I thought you meant to take me to a mantua maker's shop on Cheapside, Lady Harrington. I cannot afford to pay Mayfair prices."

"It is my wish to play fairy godmother to you today, and I shall be hurt if you refuse."

"But I must repay your kindness in some way," Sophie protested.

"You may do so in the future. Are you certain you do not have some wealthy relation — a rich uncle or aunt — who will leave you all their money after they die? Such things happen all the time in novels."

"If such a person existed in my family, I am sure my father would have told me. And he would have applied to him rather than Sir Charles."

"Then you shall give me your vowels." Lady Harrington removed a small pencil and notebook from her reticule and began to write. "Miss Sophie Moore owes The Viscountess Harrington a favor, which shall be redeemed at such a time as Lady Harrington chooses. Signed and dated this 10th day of March 1814." She handed the note and pencil to Sophie with a smile and a flourish, delighted by her ingenuity in resolving the objection. "Sign your name, if you please, Miss Moore, and your debt to me shall be official."

Sophie could not be on her high horse in the face of such high spirits. She signed her name and handed back the note, which Lady Harrington carefully folded and placed into her reticule.

Once inside the shop, Lady Harrington's eye was immediately attracted by a luxurious evening primrose-colored pelisse trimmed with white fur about the neck and sleeves. She held the long coat against Sophie and said, "You could wear this, with your dark hair and pale complexion. Most ladies cannot. But ..."

"It is too bright for someone like me."

Lady Harrington nodded and put aside the yellow-colored garment. "Your situation is an awkward one, Miss Moore. I suppose if your father had lived he would have married you off to some dashing soldier in his regiment. Perhaps we still might accomplish such a match, if you wish it."

"My dowry is not large enough even for that. I had thought instead to offer private musical instruction to young ladies."

"That is an idea, and that is why it is best you do not play too bold a part in this little masquerade we call society until we have considered all the possibilities. It is better to wait for the correct move than dash forward with a false move that cannot be corrected."

"Is London so severe?"

"More than you can imagine, Miss Moore." Lady Harrington turned her attention to a pelisse that was an elegant sea green. "This color will suit you. Shall we see if it fits?"

Sophie slipped on the coat and secured the fastenings. She did not need the long mirror standing before her to tell her that the graceful cut of the garment fitted her slim figure to perfection.

"With the right bonnet and parasol and boots and gloves, you will look as elegant as any Mayfair Miss," Lady Harrington assured her. "At least, the ones with good taste," she added.

Thanks to Lady Harrington's vast knowledge of the best shops, the expedition was a great success. All that remained was to choose a fabric for Sophie's ball gown, and once again Lady Harrington knew exactly where to find the best selection. She directed her carriage to the Pall Mall, where the linen-draper Harding Howell & Co. had its shop. However, as she was alighting from the carriage, her foot got caught and she nearly fell to the ground.

Within minutes, an entourage of shop clerks appeared on the pavement and carried her into the shop, where they gently eased her onto a sofa. Sophie followed, begging to be of some service. But Lady Harrington waved away the offers of hartshorn, tea or something more stimulating. "I have no intention of fainting," she insisted. "It is only my ankle. In a few minutes the pain will pass."

However, it did not. Indeed, with each passing minute the ankle became more swollen. At last, Lady Harrington admitted defeat.

"Miss Moore, I beg your pardon, but I fear I shall not be able to give the fabric for your dress the attention it deserves. Would you be terribly upset if we put it off for another day?"

Sophie was about to reply that her only concern was the welfare of Lady Harrington, when a high-pitched voice interrupted her.

"Lady Harrington! I am distraught! I thought I should faint when I heard the news. Did I not tell you, Lady Jane, I thought I should faint?" Miss Bryce-Jones, a tall creature with striking auburn hair and hazel eyes, was still wringing her hands from anxiety as she shot a glance in the direction of her companion, Lady Jane.

While Lady Jane nodded her head — careful to do it in such a way that the plume sitting atop her bonnet swayed gracefully above her — Lady Harrington replied, "Dear Miss Bryce-Jones, dear Lady Jane, you are both always so concerned about others."

"Shall we call a chair for you, Lady Harrington? However will you get home?" asked Lady Jane.

"Why, what a question! Your carriage is waiting outside," said Miss Bryce-Jones to the other young lady. "Do let us take you home, Lady Harrington. I am certain we do not mind giving up an hour of our morning. Do we, Lady Jane?"

Lady Jane, a blond-haired beauty with a porcelain complexion and big blue eyes — in short, an appearance that made her resemble a dainty, fashionable doll come to life — looked as though she minded very much, but she dared not say so. She and Miss Bryce-Jones were very aware that they were the leading contenders for the hand of Arthur Wentworth. To the world, they presented the picture of inseparable best friends. Privately, they both knew that the glue that bound them was jealousy and fear that the other would beat her to the finish line in the race to win the young man's affections. Lady Jane could therefore not let her rival appear to be more felicitous of Lady Harrington's wellbeing than she was, knowing that word of their respective actions would reach the Wentworth home before dinner.

"My carriage is at your disposal," Lady Jane therefore said. "Let me call my coachman."

"Thank you, but there is no need, since my carriage is also outside. However, you might do me a favor all the same." Lady Harrington beckoned to Sophie, who had been pushed into the background by the two young ladies, to step forward. "Let me introduce you to my friend, Miss Moore."

The introductions were made. By this time, Sophie was dressed from head to toe in her elegant new apparel, and the two ladies eyed her with suspicion.

"Miss Moore is visiting from Jamaica," Lady Harrington continued. "Her family is good friends with the Wentworths, and she is staying with them for the season."

Miss Bryce-Jones and Lady Jane exchanged glances.

"I had promised to help Miss Moore choose a new fabric for the gown she intends to wear to the ball in honor of Henry Wentworth's birthday celebration. Would you agree to be her guides in my stead and see her safely home?"

"With pleasure," said Miss Bryce-Jones, envisioning the happy scene when she was discussed in glowing terms in the Wentworth drawing room by Lady Harrington, with Arthur Wentworth looking on.

Lady Jane agreed to the scheme for a reason of her own.

CHAPTER V

ALTHOUGH SOPHIE DID NOT ENJOY the company of Miss Bryce-Jones and Lady Jane as much as that of Lady Harrington, she could find no fault in their attentions to her. They set the entire shop — and it was a large one — in a frenzy of activity, as though it was fabric for their own gowns that was at stake. Very soon a long counter was piled high with fabrics of every color of the rainbow, but alas, this fabric was too plain and that one had a pattern that was too ornate, while a fabric that was perfect in almost all things was regrettably too stiff, while another was just as regrettably too flimsy.

Sophie enjoyed shopping for a new dress as much as any young lady, but the morning had been a long one and so she was relieved when the three ladies finally found a fabric that they all could agree upon. After instructions had been given for the delivery of the precious package, the ladies climbed into Lady Jane's carriage.

"What a thrilling morning this has been," said Miss Bryce-Jones, adjusting her large fur muff upon her lap. "Is there anything as exciting as the hunt for just the right fabric for a new dress, or as satisfying when the fabric has finally been found? Do you not agree, Lady Jane?"

"As always, my dear Miss Bryce-Jones, you are in the right," replied Lady Jane, eying the other lady's new muff with more than a tinge of envy. Although her family was possessed of the better title, there was no question that Miss Bryce-Joyce had more pin money to spend on her clothes. Thus, Lady Jane's muff, while very fine, was not nearly as large as the muff of her friend. "However, would you not agree it is also a thrilling experience when one makes an entrance into the ballroom and all eyes turn to gaze upon your new gown?"

Miss Bryce-Jones vigorously agreed. "And you, Miss Moore?" she asked, graciously recalling there was a third person in the carriage.

Since Sophie had never been to a formal ball before, she said she could not express an opinion.

"Your first ball, Miss Moore? How too exciting!" Lady Jane exclaimed. "Then you must not breathe a word about what your gown will look like, not even to Lady Harrington. It must be a total surprise."

Sophie silently expressed an opinion such caution was unnecessary; she could not believe anyone would much care about her and what she was wearing. However, she said, "I would like to honor your request, but I do not see how I can do so. I will need to engage a dressmaker and purchase the necessary ornaments, and since I am a stranger to London I will need someone's assistance."

"It cannot be Lady Harrington," said Lady Jane. "She will need to rest her ankle for days. Let me therefore lend you my dressmaker. You can rely upon her for everything, I assure you."

"Do you not need her services for your own gown?"

"It must be that Lady Jane's gown is already finished. Have I guessed correctly?" Miss Bryce-Jones flashed a brilliant smile in her friend's direction.

Lady Jane ignored the comment, and its ungenerous implication that she might not have been so willing to share her dressmaker if her own gown was not safely completed, and said to Sophie, "Shall I have Mrs. Burns call upon you tomorrow?"

"Thank you, that is very kind of you." And Sophie was truly grateful for it had occurred to her as well that without the help of Lady Harrington she would be hard-pressed to do all that was necessary to finish the gown before the date of Henry's birthday celebration.

"Lady Jane, would you object to prolonging the pleasures of this morning by stopping at Gunter's on the way home?" asked Miss Bryce-Jones.

"An excellent suggestion — that is, if Miss Moore has no objection."

Miss Moore did not. She had no idea what sort of shop Gunter's was, but after all the two ladies had done for her that morning she had no wish to put a damper on their plans.

The carriage was directed to Berkeley Square. When they arrived, Sophie saw that their destination was a tea shop and she hesitated. Although she was still a novice to London society, she knew there were certain things a lady who wished to preserve her reputation did not do. Mrs. Hemingway had warned her several times during their long journey to England that being seen in public places such as the theatre or even the park without being properly chaperoned by a married member of the family or an abigail or other matronly companion was strictly forbidden.

"Everyone goes to Gunter's," Miss Bryce-Jones assured her, when she saw Sophie hesitate. "It is the height of respectability."

Since Lady Jane was eagerly following Miss Bryce-Jones out of the carriage, Sophie could only assume no one would find fault with her for having a cup of tea at Gunter's. And when she entered that fabled place, which enjoyed the approbation of the *ton*, she saw that her fears had been foolish. The room was crowded with elegant young ladies, all of them dressed in the latest fashions and looking as though they had just stepped out of the pages of *Ackermann's Repository.*

The three ladies were seated at a table beside a large plate-glass window that looked upon the square, the perfect setting to both see the activity on the street and to be seen by all who passed by. After their tea and cakes arrived — it was too chilly a day for the shop's exquisite ices — Sophie noticed that she was the only one who was eating. Her two companions kept their eyes upon the window.

Sophie was sure the view of the park must be delightful in the summer, when the trees were covered with green and a bright sun painted the scene with interesting contrasts of shadow and light. But due to the unseasonably cold winter and summer, the trees were bare and the park seemed to be composed of only two colors: dull gray and even duller brown.

Inside the tea shop, on the other hand, there was much to gaze upon — a riot of color, thanks to the various hues of the ladies' pelisses, as well as the imaginative bonnets and turbans that topped their heads. Sophie thought for a moment about the contrast between London and Jamaica. On the island, her home might have been plain on the inside, but she only had to step outside her front door to be greeted by a brilliant blue sky, a dazzling bouquet of wildflowers, and the ever-changing hues of the sea — a boundless display of breath-taking beauty that was absolutely free. In London, it seemed, even a brief glimpse of vibrant color could be had only for a price.

She was still absent-mindedly stirring her tea, busy with her own thoughts, when she discovered why the two ladies found the view outside the window so enthralling. Arthur Wentworth, accompanied by a stylishly dressed young man whom Sophie later learned was Miss Bryce-Smith's elder brother, passed by the window. The two gentlemen raised their hats, and Mr. Wentworth's face registered surprise at the sight of Sophie seated with the other two ladies. However, they did not stop.

"They are on their way to their boxing lesson with Gentleman Jackson, I suppose," said Miss Bryce-Jones, assuming an air of feigned innocence. "I do so worry about my brother when he goes. Last week he almost had his nose broken by Mr. Wentworth. I told Mr. Wentworth that if it should happen in earnest, I did not know if I would ever be able to forgive him."

"And what did Mr. Wentworth say to that?" asked Lady Jane, her large blue eyes narrowing into wary slits.

"Oh, you know how exasperating Mr. Wentworth can be at times. He only smiled."

"Well, if Mr. Bryce-Jones returns home with a broken nose, we shall know Mr. Wentworth's true feelings concerning you, won't we, Diana dear?"

Although Lady Jane had called the other lady by her familiar name, even Sophie, who had become acquainted with the two ladies only that morning, was aware that a malicious barb had been cast. Miss Bryce-Jones, however, was unruffled by the remark.

"Shall we? I wonder," replied the young lady, raising her teacup to her smiling lips. "Mr. Wentworth is very deep. One often feels quite at sea when one is with him. Of course, he named no names when he remarked at Lady Prudence's ball that not even the promise of good fishing in Scotland would sway him to marry a woman he did not admire — and I am certain he would never speak so insultingly about you, Lady Jane, at least not in public — but one does wonder why he chose fishing in Scotland as his example."

Miss Bryce-Jones took a sip of her tea and seemed to notice the plate of gaily iced cakes for the first time. While she expressed her delight, Lady Jane tightly clenched the handle of her parasol, her knuckles as white as her face.

The outing had lost its pleasure for Sophie, who never enjoyed displays of mean-spirited feminine rivalry, and she was relieved when the last of the tea was drunk and the carriage brought her back to the Wentworth home.

Home. It was not her home. She knew that. But already she was feeling less a stranger. She was feeling less intimidated by the grand entrance hall, with its willowy staircase that seemed to dance in a happy spiral up to the higher floors; its long Turkey carpet that was much too fine (in her opinion, if no one else's) to tread upon with muddy boots; its dazzling chandelier that seemed more suited to greeting kings and royal princesses than someone like her (or even Miss Wentworth, for that matter). She was now part of the establishment, and with her new clothes she even looked the part.

She took a moment to look into the large mirror that stood in the hall, and she liked what she saw. She was still the same Sophie Moore, but she realized that a subtle change had occurred, under Lady Harrington's skillful guidance. While there had been nothing wrong with the dress and pelisse and bonnet she brought with her from Jamaica, those garments had had too much of the "young" lady about them. Her new walking costume was more sophisticated. It had just the right touches to set off her figure, while the bonnet had a rakish slant that showed off her eyes.

Yes, she decided, there was much to admire in London. It was apparently true that London was a city where money and good taste lived in harmony, producing an offspring of luxurious elegance that was the envy of the world. But was there any real happiness, she wondered?

She thought back to Miss Bryce-Jones and Lady Jane and their rivalry over Mr. Wentworth. Did either young lady truly love the gentleman they were fighting over, or was he just another prize, on par with a new fur muff or pair of diamond earrings?

For a moment, her face flushed with anger. Neither of those ladies was deserving of Mr. Wentworth. They were too selfish, too self-absorbed. He deserved someone better, someone more ...

She stopped. She was letting her imagination run away with her again. She was confusing the Mr. Wentworth she had concocted in her daydreams with the real person. She had no idea who was the real Mr. Wentworth. His heart was a mystery to her — whether or not he could be kind, whether or not he could love, whether or not there was anything truly worth having behind that elegant exterior.

It was an interesting question, but this was not the time to dwell upon it. She had spotted a letter addressed to her sitting upon the side table where letters and visiting cards were deposited by the servants. When a closer look revealed that her letter was from Mrs. Hemingway, she eagerly took it up to her room, where she settled into a comfortable chair by the fire, looking forward to a good "coze."

The letter began in the usual way, with inquiries about Sophie's health and assurances as to the health of Mrs. Hemingway and her husband. This was followed by an interesting description of the village in Kent where Mrs. Hemingway's sister lived, a place called Sevenoaks, and Sophie could almost hear her good friend speaking to her from the written lines — a most agreeable sensation. But this was followed by a section that made Sophie pause, since it seemed to so accurately mirror her earlier thoughts:

My dear Sophie, I am happy to hear your reception by Sir Charles has been all that it should be — may the good Lord repay him amply for his kindness! Although your description of Miss Wentworth was most amusing, pray remember that in life one must make allowances. Perhaps she has known a great sorrow in her life, and it is disappointment that has soured her temperament. In any event, she is the sister of your benefactor and if only for that reason you must try to make yourself agreeable and win her affection. Also, do remember, Sophie, Miss Wentworth, and not Sir Charles, will be your most valuable ally in your quest to find employment as a music teacher, since she is much more likely to be the one to recommend you to the ladies of their circle. Therefore, do try and make an effort!

What most concerns me, though, my dear, is your silence in regard to the two sons of Sir Charles. I hope they have not insulted you by ignoring your presence, and that this is not why you do not mention them. I also hope neither one of them has treated you with disrespect, in the way some young gentlemen do when in the presence of a pretty young girl who is not of their class — a much more serious offense.

Or have you lost your heart to one of them, Sophie? Pray, write me at once and relieve me of my anxiety. Such a sentiment will only cause you great sadness, and you know I would not see you sad for a moment, if it were in my power to prevent it.

The letter ended with expressions of good wishes and assurances that Mrs. Hemingway eagerly awaited Sophie's next letter. But what could she write?

If she were to give an honest account of her day, she would have to admit it was the thought of Mr. Arthur Wentworth that had added spice to the morning's outing. At each shop, and even while she conversed with Lady Harrington, in the back of her mind she had held a silent conversation of her own: What would Mr. Wentworth think of this color, the flounce on this parasol, the ribbon on this bonnet?

Surely, though, this did not mean she had lost her heart. Surely, this only meant she missed the attention she had received at the garrison in Jamaica, the lighthearted banter she had exchanged with the soldiers, both sides knowing that the boundaries of propriety would not be overstepped, since she was just a girl barely out of the schoolroom and her father was nearby. If she thought of Mr. Wentworth, surely it could only be because he was one of the few gentlemen she had met in London, and a young lady must daydream about someone!

Sophie's thoughts went back to the tea shop and their brief meeting — their first one outside the Wentworth home. She knew he had been surprised to see her there; his momentary fluster was evidence of that. But what had it signified? Had it been an expression of displeasure — displeasure that she was seated in a fashionable tea shop as though she were on an equal footing with the members of his set? Or was it possible it had been something else, the fluster of a heretofore aloof observer who is surprised to find himself thrown unexpectedly into the role of ardent admirer?

And what had been her feelings, upon seeing him?

She blushed to recall how happy she had been.

Even now she could feel her heart start to race and her limbs turn to jelly, just because she was thinking of him. That had never happened to her before.

Was this, then, what the poets meant when they wrote of love?

No, it was too ridiculous. It was still only a mild flirtation. She only wanted him to acknowledge that she was there, a living human being, and not just part of the furniture.

No, that was not true. Not anymore.

He had seen her. And he had reflected back to her an image of herself she had never seen before, an image of a woman — a woman who was desirable in a man's eyes.

CHAPTER VI

"A HIT! A PAPABLE HIT!"

Edward Bryce-Jones glowed with pride. It wasn't often he got the better of Arthur Wentworth, and now a bright trickle of blood was making a path from the latter gentleman's nose down to his chin.

Gentleman Jackson threw a clean towel in the direction of Mr. Wentworth, who wiped the blood from his face. John Jackson, the famous boxer, was not really a gentleman of course. But that was what everyone called him. His boxing saloon on Bond Street was frequented by all of the young gentlemen belonging to the *ton*, who came there to learn the sport but also to fight off the tendency to put on weight, due to the vast quantities of rich food they consumed every day.

"Your thoughts were a hundred miles away, Mr. Wentworth," said Gentleman Jackson with disapproval. "If your mind is not on your opponent, you have no business being in the ring."

"I accept the rebuke, sir," replied Mr. Wentworth.

"Care for another round?" asked Mr. Bryce-Jones, eager to demonstrate that his win had not been a fluke.

Arthur shook his head. "I have an engagement in half an hour. I must be going."

Mr. Bryce-Jones looked about the room, eager to find another sparring partner, but only one other person was available. That person was a rather pitiable specimen, since he had a club foot. What was more, the man wrote verse! But Gentleman Jackson had succeeded in turning the poet into a respectable boxer, and so Mr. Bryce-Jones called out, "Lord Byron, care to spar with me?"

AS HE WALKED DOWN THE street, Arthur carefully rubbed his nose, which still hurt even though the bleeding had stopped. Yet, it was not the pain that bothered him. Nor was he upset that he had been beaten by Edward Bryce-Jones, who was unexceptional in every way. No, what worried him was that Gentleman Jackson had been right, at least partially. His thoughts had not been a hundred miles away, but they had not been in the ring. Instead, they had traveled the short distance to Gunter's tea shop and the sight of Miss Sophie Moore.

He had been surprised to see her there. Indeed, he found Miss Moore to be a surprising person for several reasons. Arthur Wentworth was accustomed to having women throw themselves in his path. Just a few months earlier distant relations had been guests at the Wentworth country house, and despite the enormity of the place the young lady of the family had been amazingly underfoot wherever he went, appearing in doorways and on landings of stairways with startling frequency. In town, eligible young ladies paraded themselves before him in the park and the ballroom, tried to catch his eye from their theatre boxes or from across the dining table. That his steps were being dogged by the likes of Miss Bryce-Jones and Lady Jane came as no surprise to him. But what on earth was Miss Moore doing in their company?

He sincerely hoped she was not angling after him, too. Indeed, he had found her apparent lack of interest in him to be a most pleasant change. True, she had blushed furiously, as young ladies so often did, that morning when she had flown out of the library and almost knocked him down. But she had not gotten up early, so she could meet him in the breakfast room before his morning ride in the park. Nor had she found reason to traipse down the stairs when he returned in the late afternoon to change for dinner. Best of all, she had not fainted once and upset the entire household, to the best of his knowledge.

Yet her absence did not mean she had gone unnoticed. A few times he had wandered into the library and noticed the faint scent of her fragrance lingering in the air. A book resting upon a small table in the blue sitting room showed that recently she had been there reading. Without asserting herself, Miss Moore had made her presence felt in the house.

But what was she doing at Gunter's?

Arthur had to admit that Miss Moore had looked amazingly well. The walking costume she was wearing suited her admirably. He had noticed that first night that she was attractive, but now he realized she was a true beauty. He had always been partial to dark hair, and hers was thick and lustrous, as the curls that had escaped from her bonnet showed. Although he did usually prefer blue eyes to green, he had noticed that first night when they met that there was a certain fire that glowed in those gem-like emerald eyes that was most intriguing. Her complexion was also good, and obviously someone had taken great care over the girl back in Jamaica, seeing to it that her complexion was not ruined by the burning rays of the hot sun. Yet she was no boring porcelain doll. There was a liveliness to her features that suggested a quick intellect to match.

Arthur awoke from his reverie and looked about him. To his chagrin, he had walked right past his destination. As he retraced his steps, he chided himself for once again letting Miss Moore distract him. Miss Moore was not his concern, he reminded himself. Due to the strict codes of his class, it was impossible to treat her as though she was his social equal. And due to the constraints of a gentleman's code of honor, he could not treat her as though she were just another unprotected female floundering in the dark undercurrents of London — at least not while she was enjoying the shelter of his home and the protection of his father. It was therefore best not to think of her at all, he decided.

IN A NONDESCRIPT BUILDING LOCATED on one of Mayfair's smaller and quieter streets was a boarding school for supposedly orphaned girls, although everyone knew the girls were actually the illegitimate offspring of members of society. The school had been the project of Lady Eleanor Wentworth, Arthur's mother. Upon the death of Lady Wentworth, the supervision had passed to Lady Harrington, but it was Arthur, and not Sir Charles, who paid for the school's expenses, out of the family's money. Sir Charles was the type to indulge his wife's whims, but not the type to be bothered by the details of her projects. It was enough that he had been convinced to stand for Parliament, whose sessions already took him away from his club too much.

Today, it was therefore Arthur who had to join Lady Harrington and the school's headmistress, Miss Mobley, to go over the account books.

The headmistress greeted him politely and asked if he would like to see the girls. He declined. He was no prude. He knew that liaisons unconsecrated by marriage were as common in his circle as London's gray skies and muddy streets. Still, the "fruits" of those secret, sweaty encounters were distasteful, in his opinion, and he still wondered why his mother had so eagerly and earnestly become involved with the fate of such girls, who were supposedly being educated to become governesses and equipped to earn an honest living. His mother had never revealed her reasons, but on her deathbed she had asked Arthur to promise he would continue to support the school after she was gone — and, of course, a dying mother's request was sacred.

Arthur therefore waited in the headmistress's small sitting room for the arrival of Lady Harrington. He was served tea, he drank it, and still his cousin did not arrive. He was about to suggest that he peruse the account books on his own, when a messenger from Lady Harrington appeared with a note.

Lady Harrington's writing style was as easy and flowing as her speech. She apologized to Arthur, laughed at her clumsiness, assured him there was no cause for alarm since her ankle was already much better. Arthur felt his spirits rise as he read through the letter; Lady Harrington, whether in person or in prose, always had that effect upon him.

He placed the letter in his pocket and turned his attention to the account books. When he finished, he congratulated Miss Mobley on her excellent management of the school. He had found no faults with the expenditures, which seemed to be reasonable.

"Thank you, Mr. Wentworth," Miss Mobley replied. "I have always done my best to do what is right for both the girls and your family. That is why it grieves me to have to leave the school. But my sister has become ill and she has asked me to come home to Cornwall and help take care of her children. She is a widow, sir."

"Of course, your first duty is to your family," replied Arthur, "but who will run the school?"

"I will not leave until there is someone to replace me. I was hoping to speak to Lady Harrington, sir. It is a great pity she could not be here today."

Arthur silently agreed, since he had looked forward to seeing Lady Harrington as well. But all was not lost. He assured the headmistress he would pay Lady Harrington a visit that afternoon.

CHAPTER VII

"ARTHUR, HOW KIND OF YOU to visit a wretched invalid!" Lady Harrington's face lit up at the sight of her cousin. "It was too ridiculous of me to fall, but I am paying for it dearly now. You cannot believe how bored I have been, lying here on this sofa with nothing to do except drink chocolate and read a horrid novel."

"Then it is a good thing I have brought you some news to occupy your mind," replied Arthur, taking the seat his cousin had offered him.

He had always admired his cousin Mary, but on this day he appreciated her even more than before. Whereas most other women would have made the most of an injured ankle, collapsing onto the sofa with the vapors and calling for the servants every moment to arrange the pillows, Lady Harrington was making the most of an unfortunate situation with her usual good spirits.

Of course, even if she must be banished to the sofa, that was no reason to present a frumpy appearance to the world. She was dressed in a very becoming gauzy white day dress that, Arthur noticed, was almost sheer, since it was lacking the under-garment that was usually worn under such dresses. Although large parts of the dress were covered by the long paisley shawl that was draped over her body, one could catch glimpses of her slender limbs. It was almost shocking, and he did hope she was not "at home" to other visitors while dressed in such a costume. But he could not really find fault with anything Lady Harrington did, not when her eyes were twinkling at him with real pleasure, as they were now.

Indeed, as he feasted his eyes on the lovely vision stretched out upon the sofa, he felt a pang in his heart. Although they were first cousins and had grown up together like brother and sister, he had always had a secret tendré for her. Nothing had come of it. She had always dreamed of becoming a duchess — or at least a baroness — and he could not give her that. But even though he knew the deeper feelings he felt for her would never be returned, he still judged every woman by the standard she had set for him. And he had been upset beyond words when her engagement to Lord Harrington was announced.

If ever there was a man who was unworthy of such a prize it was Lord Harrington. True, the Viscount had a good title and a fortune, but Lord Harrington was both dull and pompous. He was also already running to fat, thanks to a deep-rooted inertia that was the product of both a lazy mind and body. Arthur knew that in their set people almost never married for love, but he did not like to think of his cousin Mary trapped in an unhappy marriage for life.

Yet, Lady Harrington never showed an unhappy face to the world, and Arthur assumed she kept sadness at bay by always being engrossed in one of her "projects." He never permitted himself to consider that there might be some shallowness in her character, some lack of sensibility, which would both prevent and protect her from feeling deeply about the things in life that should matter most.

"I have a splendid idea!" said Lady Harrington, after Arthur told her about the headmistress's desire to leave her position. "What about Miss Moore?"

"Miss Moore?"

"Miss Moore is educated and has good sense, from what I can tell. And she is in want of a situation. She did mention something about giving music lessons, but there are already so many genteel ladies of dubious position doing that. The situation of headmistress will make her much more financially secure."

"But, Mary, we have no idea if Miss Moore is capable of running a school."

"I am certain there is not much to it. Besides, no one really cares about the girls and their education. And if Miss Moore accepts the position — and I do not see how she can refuse — it will save us the bother of having to find someone to replace Miss Mobley."

Even though he could not find fault with his cousin's logic, Arthur felt curiously irritated by the superficial way his cousin was treating the problem.

"I shall ask Miss Moore to come here — it is such a bother not being able to walk because of this ankle. I think I can explain to her most of the duties, but you shall have to discuss the money with her, Arthur. You know so much more about that than I do. Do you think we should speak to Miss Moore together, or separately? Perhaps it will be best if I speak to her first, so she can become accustomed to the idea. I shall write to her at once."

Lady Harrington paused, as a new thought entered her mind. "And perhaps Aunt Dorothea was right after all. Perhaps I should not have taken Miss

Moore to all the finest shops to do her shopping. Her new clothes are beautiful, but hardly suitable for the headmistress of a boarding school for orphaned girls."

Lady Harrington turned her head toward the writing desk that sat at the end of the room. "Be a dear, Arthur, and bring me pen and ink," she said, settling back upon the sofa. When he went to do her bidding, she smiled a little smile, one that was only for her.

However, when Arthur returned, it was not with pen and ink, but a frown. "I would prefer we found someone more experienced, Mary. My mother always tried to find the very best people for the school. I would like to continue that tradition."

Although inwardly Lady Harrington was not pleased — she had never liked Lady Eleanor Harrington, since she found that lady to be entirely too serious — she did not let her irritation show. Instead, she smiled up at him and said, "Whatever you wish, Arthur."

AFTER LEAVING LADY HARRINGTON, ARTHUR went to his club, as he usually did in the afternoon. Indeed, White's was like a second home to him, and he sank down into a comfortable wing chair with relief. His head was throbbing. He blamed it upon the blow he had received at the boxing saloon and the approaching storm; rainstorms usually announced their presence as a headache before he felt the first raindrop.

His spirits did not improve when Poggy Makepeace plopped himself down in the wing chair next to his. "Hullo, Wentworth. Care to take a look at these sparklers and tell me what you think?"

Poggy — the nickname was used so universally there was hardly anyone who remembered the young man's real name — took out a jeweler's box and opened the lid. A diamond and ruby brooch sat inside.

"Very nice. Is it for your fiancée?"

"Of course not," said Poggy, offended. "Mother's jewels will take care of that. It's for Miss Grant, the actress. Do you think she will like it?"

"How should I know what Miss Grant will like?"

"I thought ... well, that's what people said."

Arthur shrugged. He did not like to discuss his private affairs with just anyone. Although Poggy was a member of the club, he was not one of Arthur's intimate friends.

"I hear she is very difficult to please," said Poggy, staring down at the brooch. "I hear she throws things, if she does not like them."

"Is that Miss Grant you are talking about?" Another member of the club joined them. "If it is, you are too late, Poggy."

"Too late?"

"Lord Shrewsbury and Miss Grant came to terms this morning. She was parading around the park in her new carriage just now."

Poggy's jaw fell open, giving him the dumbfounded look that had inspired his nickname. The other young gentleman laughed and walked away.

"I suppose I may as well return this," said Poggy, closing the lid of the box.

"Cheer up, Poggy. Miss Grant is not the only actress in London," said Arthur.

"You are right." The young man's face brightened. "I am going to the Drury Lane tonight. Perhaps I'd better bring this brooch along."

Poggy drifted off. Arthur returned to gazing gloomily into the fire. He never thought the day would come when he would envy someone like Poggy Makepeace, but at least Poggy was not bored with life as he was.

A few short years ago, he might have been excited by the news of a beautiful new actress showing off her charms on stage — and stimulated by the chase to win her favors. But after a few brief liaisons, the dance of conquest, as well as victory, had become as predictable and wearisome as last season's play.

His cousin Mary had been the only woman who had been able to retain his interest. Now that she was married, they had been forced to curtail their meetings and he found the days when they did not meet to be impossibly dull. Lately, even when they did meet, those meetings left him feeling restless and dissatisfied with life.

He wandered into another room of the club, where some card tables were set up. It was too early for the real heavy betters to make an appearance, but already there were a few players huddled about a table, grasping their cards as though their lives depended upon it. Since some of those players were addicted to the game, and had already gambled away much of their fortunes, perhaps their lives did depend upon those grimy pieces of paper they were clutching so tightly.

"You look like you could use a glass of punch."

Arthur felt a hand clasp his shoulder. He turned and took up the suggestion with relief. George Somerton was an old friend from school. Like Arthur, he was the elder son of a baronet, and so they had always felt as though they had something in common. After they claimed a table and ordered a bowl of punch, they settled in for a comfortable hour of talk and drink.

"The war cannot last much longer," said Somerton. "I suppose you have heard the news. Wellington has captured Bordeaux."

Arthur nodded. "Are you sorry to have missed it? The fighting?"

"I am not sorry I have not had my legs blown away by one of Boney's cannons — or been killed, for that matter. I would like to enjoy my life."

"And do you?"

Somerton gave him an odd glance. "Dropped too much at the gaming tables? I can give you a loan, if you like."

"Nothing like that," said Arthur, with a laugh. "I am just feeling a bit at loose ends, at the moment."

"I know the feeling, like you want to join an expedition going down the Amazon River or go the South Seas."

"Yes, something like that."

"People who do that usually end up badly, Wentworth. If they are not eaten by the natives, they catch some infernal, incurable disease and end their days unable to do anything except yell at the servants, swallow vile potions and write their memoirs."

"I forgot that you have an uncle who traveled with Cook."

"A cousin, actually."

"I suppose he has some interesting tales about his adventures in the South Seas."

"Yes, but unfortunately he has being boring everyone to tears with them for the last twenty years."

Somerton refilled their glasses. The punch was strong. It was also warm and mellow enough to cast a contemplative haze over Arthur's spirits.

"What then makes for a good life?" he asked his companion. "If our lot is not to be soldiers or explorers, how do we, the elder sons of England, make our mark upon the world?"

"Politics?"

Arthur shook his head. From Sir Charles he had learned that most of an MP's time was spent snoring on a back bench. Only a very few exceptional men truly made a difference when it came to charting the course of the country.

"Does it really matter?" asked Somerton. "Why is it not enough to enjoy life — the food, the drink, the ladies?"

"Is that not how an animal lives?"

Somerton took a long drink from his glass. "Your problem, Wentworth, is that you think too much. You have too much imagination. A dangerous thing, too much imagination. Better to keep your eye on ... on ... on what a man can see with his own eyes."

Somerton's speech was starting to become slightly slurred, but he was also starting to warm to his subject. Unlike Arthur, he had once been interested in having a political career, talked about one day being prime minister. Now, he slammed his open tankard down on the table, as though he were addressing a public meeting and wished to bring home an important point, and some of the liquid splattered his white cravat and dribbled down his waistcoat. "Wentworth, we have a duty to enjoy our privileges as elder sons. If we start moping and talking about being dissatisfied, what will be with the common people? Who will fight our wars, and get themselves killed so we can go on having a good dinner, if we start going around saying the dinner isn't worth it? Answer me that."

Arthur replied by pushing the punch bowl in his companion's direction, and left Somerton to his drink.

White's, the most fashionable gentlemen's club in London, today seemed very small; its regimen of gambling, drinking and gossiping felt too constricting. He went outside, with no purpose in mind. But, London was a vast metropolis. Perhaps the city would take pity upon him, a too privileged elder son, and surprise him by throwing an adventure his way.

CHAPTER VIII

ALAS, IT WAS NOT MEANT to be. He had not left White's two minutes when he heard himself being hailed by a familiar, unwelcome voice.

"Wentworth, tell my sister it is true," Edward Bryce-Jones called out to him. "Did I bloody your nose or not?"

Arthur lifted his hat to Miss Bryce-Jones and Lady Jane. "Your brother is progressing admirably, Miss Bryce-Jones. He very nearly knocked me out."

"How terrible!" Lady Jane exclaimed. "I hope you were not mortally hurt."

"Hardly, ma'am, since I am talking to you."

Arthur was about to excuse himself, when Mr. Bryce-Jones, heeding a nudge in the ribs from his sister, said, "What about us having a look at those new prints of yours? That is, of course, if you are free."

The last thing Arthur wanted to do was spend a quarter of an hour listening to the two ladies extoll the virtues of pictures they neither understood nor cared about. But at a dinner party he had made the fatal mistake of mentioning he had purchased some watercolor sketches by J.M.W. Turner and so he could not now refuse showing them.

The small party therefore repaired to the Wentworth home. Refreshments were brought for the guests. Arthur did his best to explain why the watercolors were exceptional, and not just daubs of color on paper, as Miss Bryce-Joyce had so eloquently expressed her judgment of them, while every few minutes he glanced at the clock, wondering when the social call might be civilly concluded.

SOPHIE WAS IN THE BLUE sitting room playing the harp when she heard the voices of the two ladies. She heard Arthur's voice as well. But much as she longed to join the group, she knew she would not be welcome.

However, she could not return to her playing. Just knowing that Mr. Wentworth was in the house was enough to make her restless and unable to concentrate. She found herself wondering if, after his guests were gone, he might come into the sitting room — for what reason she did not know. If he did, would he speak to her? For once, would she know what to say? And how absurd it was that she could not see his face or hear his voice without regressing into a silly schoolroom miss!

Since she could not concentrate on her playing, she decided to do some embroidery work instead. Her work basket was upstairs, in her room. There, at least, she need not worry about Mr. Wentworth coming upon her unexpectedly and sending her into a blushing fit.

On her way to the staircase, she passed the library, whose door was open. She noticed that the furniture closest to the fireplace was covered with sheets, and she recalled Miss Wentworth mentioning at breakfast that a chimney sweep would be cleaning out some of the fireplaces, including the one in the library. She did not see the man — perhaps he was down in the kitchen — but as she turned to continue down the hallway, she thought she heard the sound of a muffled cry.

She turned back and stood in the doorway, listening for a few moments. She heard only silence. Thinking she had been mistaken, she again turned toward the door — and again heard a cry. This cry was followed by the sound of something falling from the chimney and landing in the fireplace with a thud.

Her first thought was that Henry Wentworth was playing another one of his tricks. Then she recalled he was not at home. At any rate, he would not know when she might enter the library and he obviously would not lie in wait for her for hours.

The sound of more debris falling made her approach the fireplace, and for the third time she heard a cry. This time she was certain the sound was coming from somewhere up in the chimney, and her heart began to beat a little faster. She knew that very young boys were apprenticed to chimney sweeps and expected to climb up into the narrow places that the adult sweep could not reach with his brushes and brooms. She wondered if one of those children was up in the chimney now.

"Hello?" she called out. Sticking her head inside the fireplace and turning it so that she was looking up into the dark expanse, she said, "Are you all right?"

She was answered by several small clumps of soot that fell onto her face. She recalled she had left her handkerchief in the blue sitting room, and so she had only her hands to use to wipe the soot from her eyes. Regarding her filthy hands, and wondering what her face must look like, she decided that perhaps it would have been better not to get involved. But then she heard again the sound of a child crying, and the sound of it rent her heart.

"Are you hurt?" she called out. When there was no answer, she said, "You can tell me. I won't tell your master." When there was still no answer, she said, "Please, at least tell me your name."

"William," a small voice answered. It sounded very far away. "Mum," the small voice added.

"William, is something wrong? Can I be of assistance?"

There was no answer, but there was the sound of a movement and then some more soot fell into Sophie's eyes. The boy again began to cry.

"William, I wish to help you. Please, tell me why you are crying."

"I'm afraid."

Sophie could very well imagine that the child was afraid, stuck as he was in the dark chimney. But she was not sure how she could help. She could hardly climb up and get him; the opening was much too narrow.

"William, do you wish to come down?"

"I can't."

"Why not?"

"I don't know how." The child again began to sob. This time the cries came loud and quick, as though the child's despair was so great that he no longer cared who heard him.

"William, try to be brave. Do you remember how you climbed up? Was there a place to put your hands and feet?"

She heard something that she hoped was a yes. "Try to find the foothold. Slowly. Have you found it?"

"Yes, mum."

"There should be another one, below it. Have you found it?"

After a few moments, the child replied that he had. Sophie encouraged the boy to slowly find the places for his hands and feet, and in this way the child gradually descended. But when he was still somewhere in the chimney he missed the foothold and gave a scream that filled the room. Sophie held out her hands to try to catch the falling child. When William did reach her waiting arms, the force of his fall made her lose her balance and she knocked her head against the fireplace wall. But at least the child was safe. She sank down onto the floor, cradling in her arms the still-sobbing child, who appeared to be no older than five or six.

"What a sight you look, Miss Moore!" said Miss Bryce-Jones, breaking into peals of laughter.

Apparently William's scream had filled not just the library, but the entire house, and sent at least some of the occupants running into the library.

"Is that Miss Moore? I thought she was one of those Jamaican slaves!" said Lady Jane, also laughing.

"Can you not see the child is in distress?" Sophie cried. "Get out! All of you!"

The two young ladies, who were unaccustomed to being addressed in such a manner, were so shocked that their laughter immediately died away. Mr. Bryce-Jones was about to come to the defense of his sister, when a sharp look from Arthur stopped him.

"You will forgive me if I do not escort you to the door, ladies." He made a bow in their direction and Mr. Bryce-Jones escorted them out of the room.

He then turned back to Sophie, who had scrambled to her feet, while the child clung to her skirt. "I assume your order to clear the room did not include me, Miss Moore."

"No," she murmured.

"Perhaps you would like to explain what this is about?"

"This child was stuck in the chimney, and afraid. I tried to help him get out."

"It did not occur to you to call for his master?"

"No, it did not," Sophie replied, her eyes flashing with anger. "His master would have given the child a severe beating for making a fuss. You know that, as well as I do."

"The sweep belongs to his master. You should not have interfered."

"We are not talking about a broom, Mr. Wentworth. We are speaking of a child. Although he may be an orphan, his is still a creation of the Almighty, as much as you are."

"I stand rebuked for my choice of words," said Arthur. "May I ask what you intend to do now?"

Sophie could feel the boy clutching even more tightly at her skirt. She knew William was terrified by the thought of having to return to his master, the chimney sweep, and rightly so. Jamaica was full of slave plantations. Some of the masters had not been cruel, but she had heard tales about those who were, seen the scars on a slave's face. The chimney sweep might not be master of a large planation, but in his own dominion he would probably be just as cruel. She shuddered to think of the punishment that awaited William.

But what could she do? If she were rich as Miss Bryce-Jones or Lady Jane, she could purchase William's freedom from the chimney sweep. But she had so little money of her own, and her own future was so uncertain. Yet, she knew what her father would have done. Once, when he had seen a plantation owner mercilessly beat a child, he had thrown some money in the man's face and taken the boy away. Sophie could not remember what had happened to the child afterward; she had been very young herself. But she seemed to recall that her father had arranged for the boy to learn a trade with a kinder master. Perhaps she could do the same for William, and she said as much to Mr. Wentworth.

"Do you intend to purchase the freedom of every child in London who works as a chimney sweep, Miss Moore? I warn you, there must be hundreds of them."

"My father taught me that a person does not have to solve every problem in the world, but when one lands at his door it is a sign from heaven that it is his responsibility to rectify it."

Arthur was silent. Then he looked down at the child, who was peering up at him with large eyes from behind Sophie's soot-covered skirt. "Young man, do you know what a bath is?"

The child shook his head in the negative and slipped even further behind Sophie for protection.

"His name is William," Sophie murmured.

Arthur nodded and said, "William, if you are very brave and do not cry during the bath you are about to receive, you shall find a good dinner waiting for you afterward. Do you think you can endure sitting in a tub of hot water without screaming your head off?"

"I can try, sir."

"That is a fair answer." Arthur went to the bell pull and a few moments later a servant appeared at the door.

The servant was exceptionally well-trained. He neither blanched at the sight of Sophie, nor did he lift an eyebrow when he was instructed to take charge of the child. The one thing he did do was keep a careful distance, so that soot would not rub off on his livery.

When they were gone, Arthur said, "I will pay the chimney sweep for William's freedom and inform the kitchen staff to find some work for the boy. Will that satisfy you?"

"Yes. Thank you, Mr. Wentworth."

Arthur bowed and left.

Sophie, now alone in the room, exhaled a deep breath. She did not know from where she had gotten the courage to stand up to Mr. Wentworth, but she was glad she had been able to do so, for the child's sake. She was also glad she been allowed a glimpse into Mr. Wentworth's heart — and discovered that he did indeed have one.

However, the glimpse she caught of her reflection in the mirror afforded her no such satisfaction. In short, she gasped. Her face and the bodice of her gown were almost completely covered with dark smudges of soot. Her hair was also a fright, since the front curls were in total disarray. She was devastated — no, horrified was the better word — that this was the picture she had just presented to Mr. Wentworth.

Then her eyes traveled to the reflected doorway. Arthur Wentworth was standing there, watching her and apparently enjoying every moment of her discomfort. He smiled, bowed a second time, and then he disappeared.

CHAPTER IX

IT WAS SEVERAL DAYS LATER, and once again Sophie was regarding her reflection in the mirror. This time, she could enjoy the sight. Her new gown for the ball was even more beautiful than she had hoped for. The dressmaker, Mrs. Burns, had truly been a godsend; and for the first time since the feverish round of activity had begun, even that lady allowed a small smile to flit across her face.

"You are a genius. A wizard! I do hope the gown will not disappear at the stroke of midnight," Sophie exclaimed.

"I should think you are quite safe on that account, Miss Moore. Pray stand still while I adjust the ribbons on the bodice.

Sophie had no objection. It was the satin ribbon along the neckline and the ones that flowed down the bodice to the Empire waistline like shimmering streams that had added just the right touch of elegance to the puce-colored, gently patterned dress.

After the fitting session had concluded, Mrs. Burns packed up the dress and returned to her workshop to do the final alterations. Sophie tried to sit quietly at her writing desk and finish her letter to Mrs. Hemingway, but she was much too excited. She had accepted Sir Charles's invitation to play the harp and she knew that tomorrow night Arthur Wentworth would not absent himself from the house, not when the ball was being held in honor of his younger brother.

If Mrs. Hemingway could have seen her at that moment, Sophie knew the good woman would most likely be shocked to see Sophie so deliriously happy at the thought of being seen and admired. But Mrs. Hemingway was far away in Kent, and so Sophie decided to allow herself to be excited and happy and enjoy every minute of preparation before her first formal ball. What would come of it all on the morrow, she would discover soon enough.

Downstairs, the house had been turned upside down in happy chaos. Sophie thought she might not be in the way if she chose a quiet corner of the ballroom to stand in and watch the preparations. She therefore slipped down the stairs and found a position from where she could observe all the activity.

The ballroom was not large by country house standards, but it was more than ample for a private ball. The servants had already rolled up the great Turkey carpet, and the highly polished, inlaid wood floor was revealed. But to Sophie's surprise, a group of workers were on their hands and knees and drawing elaborate designs on the floor with pieces of chalk.

Henry had spotted her and come to stand beside her. Since she did not mind showing her ignorance before him, she asked, "Why are they doing that to your beautiful floor?"

"Like many beautiful things, it is also treacherous," he replied. "One false move on that polished surface and a lady could go flying and land in a most compromising position. Since my father has no wish to shock my aunt, he has hired artisans to chalk the floor. The chalk prevents slippages." Henry then added, "I assume you dance, Miss Moore?"

"I am familiar with some dances. I am curious to see how London ladies and gentlemen will perform them."

"You enjoy watching, then?"

"Very much."

"That is a lucky thing. You see, you may not have a partner for every dance, or even many of them. It will not be such a large ball, and ..."

"No one will wish to dance with a young lady who has no fortune?"

"I did not say you would not have any partners. I hope you will not refuse me a dance, Miss Moore."

"I shall be honored to dance with you, Mr. Wentworth," she said, and she meant it. She knew he had spoken not to hurt her, but to prepare her for the slight he felt was almost certain to come. Someone in her situation usually would spend most of the evening sitting at the side of the room, with the elderly women and the matrons who would be zealously watching their unmarried daughters shine on the dance floor.

Yet she had hope, after what had passed between her and Arthur Wentworth the afternoon when they had rescued William, that Mr. Wentworth would ask her to be his partner for one set. The rules of the ballroom would not allow for more, but even one dance would make her gloriously happy—however, she kept this thought to herself.

Henry, feeling he had done his duty to Miss Moore by explaining the social intricacies of a ball and wishing very much to now change the subject, said, "My, this conversation has turned solemn. Shall we not talk about more frivolous things during these last few hours of my minority? You have been most secretive about your new gown, Miss Moore, which, I must tell you, is highly unusual. A young lady is supposed to be thinking of nothing else besides her new dress before a ball, and disturbing the thoughts of everyone around her, too, with her incessant chatter. Are you really so indifferent to the charms of a new dress? Can it be that such a woman truly exists?"

"I have no wish to lie to you, or pretend to be better than I am. My new dress has been foremost in my mind for these past several days, sir."

"Then why do you not speak of it?"

"I ..." Sophie was about to say she wished her new gown to be a surprise, but she realized this would sound absurd to Henry. From his earlier words she knew that in his opinion no one at the ball would care what she wore. She therefore said, trying her best to assume a light air to match his, "Because I have no charming Wentworth sister to confide in. It is most inconsiderate of you, Mr. Wentworth, to not have a younger sister my age."

"That complaint you must leave at my father's feet. Though I do not know what we should do if I had one, since there is already an extra lady for my ..." Henry stopped in mid-sentence and blushed.

Sophie was struck momentarily silent too. She was certain she knew what Henry had meant to say, that there was an extra, unaccompanied lady invited to the birthday dinner before the ball — herself. But rather than be mortified by the situation, and the embarrassment her unwelcome presence was apparently causing in some quarters at what was meant to be a family dinner before the more public entertainment began, her thoughts were busy sorting out another problem. She had promised Lady Jane she would not reveal her new dress to anyone before the ball. It was a silly promise, but she had made it and she did not like to break her word. However, she could not create a grand entrance in the ballroom if the family had already seen the dress in the dining room. Therefore, the solution to the family's conundrum about dinner was happily also the solution to her problem about the ballroom.

"Mr. Wentworth, would you be offended if I did not join you and your guests for dinner, and instead had a light meal in my room?"

"I should say I would be offended, Miss Moore!" Henry vigorously protested. "Just because I am the biggest blunder head in England does not mean you should not join us at table."

"But you would really be doing me a great kindness. I shall be so nervous—the ball, the other guests you have invited to dinner ..."

"There is nothing to be afraid of. You already know Lady Harrington. I have never heard her husband speak more than six words to anyone at these affairs, so there is nothing to take offence at if he says just three words to you, one of which is certain to be 'Ah.' As for the rest of the family, well, I should try to stay away from Lady Carr. She can be demanding. But the others are as most relations are, I suppose."

"Still, if I truly did prefer to eat a light dinner in my room, would you make my excuses to Sir Charles and inform Miss Wentworth?"

"If that is your command, I shall of course obey your wishes. But in return, you must not forget about the dance you have promised me, to show you truly are not offended by my blunder."

"I am sure no one could be offended by you for very long. I shall look forward to our dance with pleasure."

Henry bowed and left to perform his errand. As he was walking down the corridor, in search of his aunt, who was supervising all the details of the event, he saw his brother Arthur.

"Well, that is one problem solved. Miss Moore prefers to have a light meal in her room before the ball."

"Have we treated her so badly that she now abhors the sight of us all?"

"I have not asked her to polish the silver, if that is what you mean." Henry let out a sigh of frustration. "I like Miss Moore well enough, but it is a devilishly difficult thing to have a conversation with her. One is always saying something one should not. But, Arthur, you will ask her to dance, won't you? It is only a private ball. Your luster won't be dulled by dancing with a nobody."

"I hope I know my duties as a host," Arthur replied.

Arthur continued on his way down the hall. Henry stared after him, offering a silent prayer that when he reached the age of twenty-five he hoped he would not be as insufferable as his brother.

Yet, Arthur was not feeling as insufferable as his outward demeanor might suggest. He too had been thinking about the ball—and the pleasure he was pretty sure he was going to receive when dancing with the very original, very pretty Miss Moore.

CHAPTER X

BEFORE THERE COULD BE PLEASURE, though, first there was duty. Every family has its formidable creature, the person who no one particularly likes, but no one dares to offend. As Henry had mentioned to Sophie, in the Wentworth family that person was Lady Carr.

She was an aunt of Sir Charles and already quite ancient. She had buried not only a husband, but also all of her children who had survived into adulthood: two sons who had died on the battlefield and one daughter who had died in childbirth. She therefore had no direct heirs, but many relations, all of whom hoped she would remember them in her will — she had a fortune in her own right that she was free to bestow upon whoever she pleased — when that time came.

Because Lady Carr had been in Bath for much of the winter, and therefore had not opened her own townhouse in London, she informed Sir Charles that he would have the pleasure of her company not only at the ball for Henry, but that she would stay at his home for a few days afterward. Thus, the servants were busy with both getting ready for the birthday celebration and preparing for the great lady's arrival.

Those preparations had not overly affected Sophie, although her maid Joan had been assigned to first see to the needs of Lady Carr, before attending to Miss Moore. Sophie did not mind. She understood that Lady Carr must come first, not only because of her title and fortune but also because of her great age.

Sophie had thought it best to remain in her room during the hour of the lady's arrival. But through her closed door, she could hear the hustle and bustle and imagine all that was going on. Numerous trunks were carried up the stairs, followed several minutes later by Lady Carr and Miss Wentworth, who was speaking with a subservient tone of voice that Sophie had never heard before.

"We hope you will find your room comfortable, Lady Carr. It is the one with the most sun. ... You do not like the morning sun? Then, of course, we shall tell the servants not to open the curtains in the morning. ... The name of the servant who will be attending you? Her name is Joan. ... You do not like the name Joan? ... Oh, I quite agree. Jane is a much better name for a maid. I cannot think why all servants are not named Jane. ... What? ... Not the male servants, of course. I did not mean the male servants. ..."

The slow procession finally reached Lady Carr's room, and the voices faded away. Sophie went back to the book she had been reading, a collection of ghost stories translated from the French and called *Tales of the Dead*. A few minutes later, though, a very apologetic Joan entered her room, followed by two other servants.

"Beg your pardon, miss, but Lady Carr is distressed there is not a library couch in her room, and Miss Wentworth says we should take this one."

Since Sophie had never used the couch, she assured Joan that she would not miss it. A moment later, there was the sound of a hand bell furiously ringing.

The two servants, followed by an anxious Joan, quickly carried the couch out of the room.

During the next several minutes, there was quite a bit of noise in the corridor as servants scurried back and forth; very likely the great lady had found other things about the room that displeased her. Sophie also heard the voices of the family members, and it seemed that the hub of family life had moved from the downstairs rooms to the one belonging to Lady Carr. Rather than be annoyed by the noise, Sophie found it to be a welcome change from the almost sepulcher-like silence that had reigned in the house until then, although she was very grateful she would not be required to bow and scrape to Lady Carr.

However, she had only just finished congratulating herself upon this fact, when Miss Wentworth appeared at her door, and said, "Lady Carr would like you to join us, Miss Moore."

Sophie could not imagine why she was wanted, but she followed Miss Wentworth down the hall. When she entered, she saw that Sir Charles and Arthur and Henry were seated around Lady Carr, who was the center of their attention.

Lady Carr was even more formidable than Sophie had imagined. She was a large woman, and had strong, almost masculine features. Although it was doubtful she had ever been a beauty, she had an erect carriage and commanding air, which suggested that she had gotten her way in life without having to resort to the usual feminine wiles.

After the introduction was made, Sir Charles said, "I was just telling Lady Carr that you are musical."

"I want someone to read to me, not hurt my ears by pounding away on a pianoforte," said Lady Carr.

"Yes, well, it is almost the same thing. The arts ..."

Sophie came to his rescue and said, "I shall be delighted to read to you, Lady Carr."

"Mind, this does not mean I have agreed to engage you."

Sophie gave Sir Charles a puzzled look, but it was Lady Carr who answered.

"I am looking for a new companion. Do you play piquet?"

"I do not play cards, Lady Carr."

"Because you do not know how to win, or because you are afraid to lose?"

"Because I think cards are a waste of time."

"I suppose you think reading the scandal sheets is a waste of time, too."

"Of course, Lady Carr."

"Then you won't do."

Lady Carr turned away and began to talk to Sir Charles. Sophie, assuming she had just been dismissed, turned towards the door with relief. She felt as though she had just been thrown into the Lion's Den, and miraculously found a trap door through which to escape. Never mind, that she was not the bluestocking Lady Carr was probably imagining; the main thing was that if Lady Carr did not wish to employ her, the family would not press Sophie to accept a position for which she was so entirely unsuited.

"I did not say you could go."

There was an uncomfortable pause as Sophie considered how to respond.

"Miss Moore is a guest, Lady Carr, not a servant," said Arthur. "If you would like someone to read to you later on, you may ask one of the servants to see if Miss Moore is available."

Lady Carr snorted. "And if she is not, should I send for you?"

"I am at your service, ma'am, although I doubt our tastes in literature are alike."

"I doubt we have similar tastes in anything, Mr. Wentworth," said Lady Carr, casting a disdainful glance at Arthur and then, with growing interest, at Sophie. However, when she spoke it was to Henry. "You shall be my piquet companion while I am here. And if you succeed in amusing me, as you usually do, I might let you win a hand or two."

SOPHIE SAT BY THE FIRE, almost dozing. A light rain was tapping against her window, and the cheerful flames made her feel safe and warm. She had spent a splendid few hours dreaming about Arthur Wentworth, luxuriating in the memory of the way he had come to her defense in Lady Carr's room. That encounter had expanded, until it was no longer a short exchange, but an entire adventure, complete with crumbling castle, weird sounds that disturbed the quiet of the night, and an evil queen in deadly battle with her rivals, the captive princess and the young and gallant prince who was the true heir to the throne.

It was a happy dream, but the hour was getting late. Through the closed door, she could hear muffled sounds from below. The other guests were arriving for Henry's birthday dinner.

Joan entered with a tray and set it down upon a table.

"Shall I return in an hour, miss, to help you dress?"

"Yes, that will be fine."

"It is exciting, isn't it, miss?"

"Yes, it is."

"We're being allowed to watch part of the dancing from the old musicians' gallery. And cook has prepared a special supper for us down in the kitchen." Joan then added, "This is my first ball. I've always dreamed of seeing one."

"Were you not here for Mr. Wentworth's twenty-first birthday?"

"No, miss. I only went into service a year ago."

"What did you do before?"

"My mother had a millinery shop, and I helped her make the hats. But after she passed away there were so many debts that I couldn't continue."

Joan left. That life could be difficult, Sophie already knew. A person needed inner strength to survive life's succession of pounding waves that tried to beat a person down. Sophie decided that if she were ever rich, she would not be like Lady Carr, who most assuredly was like a pounding wave. Instead, she would help Joan start a new millinery shop. Why shouldn't a person be allowed to pursue their dreams?

The aroma of tasty food that was rising from the tray reminded Sophie she should eat her dinner while that food was still hot. But she was at once too comfortable in her chair and too keyed up to think about anything as mundane food. After all, this was her first ball, too.

Of course, she too had watched from a gallery the dancing below when there had been a dance in Jamaica. The soldiers had been dashing in their splendid uniforms and the ladies had been beautiful. Now, she had her own beautiful dress — and a young man who she wished to please. And this was London! The most magical city in the world!

In another hour, some of that magic would be hers.

CHAPTER XI

SIR CHARLES BEAMED AS HE walked about the crowded ballroom, greetings his guests and attending to their comfort. He found chairs for the elderly women, offered to bring glasses of punch to the matrons, and of course lavishly complimented the beauty and grace of the daughters. There were servants who could have performed the first two tasks, and indeed liveried footmen darted about the room. But Sir Charles prided himself upon being both a generous and convivial host; there was none of the nose-in-the-air baronet pretending to be a duke about him.

"It is going well, is it not, Mary?" he said to Lady Harrington. "Ah, there is Miss Appleby. Charming young lady. Looks just like her mother did, when she was sixteen."

"It is a pity she has no fortune." Lady Harrington eyed the girl's dress, a delicate gown of white muslin, soft as a cloud, which was given interest by an intricately embroidered white-on-white floral garland that cascaded down from the gathered waist to the hem of her skirt. She voiced her surprise that Miss Appleby's dressmaker was still extending credit to the family, since the extent of her father's debts was well known.

"Appleby may inherit someday," Sir Charles reminded her.

"If he does not die before the Duke of Merton. I hear the Duke intends to live to be one hundred."

Lady Harrington went off to speak to some friends of hers, while Sir Charles went to greet the guests who were just arriving.

The young people took their places in the middle of the floor, for the first dance, and the musicians began to play.

Henry danced the first set with Miss Appleby. Arthur was partnering a lady who had been on the marriage market for six years and still not found a husband — although the title was good, the family's fortune was not — and this was always a tricky situation. A gentleman had to maintain a flow of conversation throughout the dance set, which might last anywhere from thirty minutes to a full hour, without raising the hopes of the lady that there was more to his attentions than ordinary politeness. Miss Thornhope, however, proved to be unusually talkative.

"Your brother and Miss Appleby make a charming couple. But how fleeting youth is! How quickly we ladies fade." She cast a knowing look to the right, in the direction of Miss Bryce-Jones, and then turned her gaze to the left and the other dancers. "And there is dear Lady Jane. Her dress is charming, but she will never see sixteen again."

Arthur was tempted to add, "Some of us will never see twenty-four again, either." But, as always, he was the perfect gentleman. He would neither stoop to catch Miss Thornhope's bait nor cast a line of his own. Besides, Miss Thornhope was keeping the conversation going without his help. Her gaze had fallen upon Lady Harrington, and she said, "Lady

Harrington is the one woman who never seems to age. Even marriage to the dullest man in England has not dimmed her glowing looks. Of course, some people say there is a reason for her happiness, that now she is safely married and has gotten her title, she can have her little love affairs — and we all know what a secret love affair can do for a lady's complexion."

"You are speaking about my cousin, ma'am."

Miss Thornhope gave him yet another of her knowing looks. "And I am speaking as a friend. People are beginning to talk, Mr. Wentworth. They wonder why you do not marry. Some are even saying it is because you and Lady Harrington have such a comfortable arrangement that you do not feel the need for a wife."

Arthur retained his unfazed demeanor, but inside he was seething. If a man had said those words, he would have known how to respond. But he could hardly challenge Miss Thornhope to a duel. He could not even insult her by walking away and leaving her unaccompanied in the middle of the dance floor. That would only set tongues wagging even more. He therefore forced himself to remain civil while he changed the topic and asked, "Have you seen Kean's Hamlet? They say he is rather good."

"If I were Ophelia, I should not drown myself for Mr. Kean. He is much too short to play the hero."

"Then it is just as well you are not that lady, Miss Thornhope. It would quite ruin the play."

SOPHIE GAVE ONE LAST LOOK into the mirror. Her dress, her hair — everything was perfect. She floated out of her room as though in a dream.

When she came to the stairway, she could hear the muffled sounds of music and laughter and the mingling tones of animated conversation. To her ears, it sounded like a symphony of joy, and she smiled to think that tonight she herself would be a note in that happy composition.

At the bottom of the stairs she could see spilling out into the corridor light from the ballroom's dazzling chandeliers. She allowed herself to be carried along by the noise and the light, still floating as though she were being magically transported by a cloud.

The doorway was before her. She was there. Her first ball! Magical, magical London!

But something was wrong. It was not just that the music had stopped; she had arrived just as the first set was over. All the other noise had slowly died away too — the talk, the laughter.

And everyone was looking at her, as though they were seeing a ghost.

"Good Lord," she heard Lady Carr exclaim, the voice ringing loud and clear in the unnaturally silent room.

IT WAS SIR CHARLES WHO first broke the spell. He came forward and took Sophie by the arm. "Miss Moore, you are here at last. Let me offer you a glass of punch."

He looked about for a servant but spotted Henry first. "Henry, find a chair for Miss Moore. I mean a glass of punch."

"But ..."

Sir Charles whispered something into Henry's ear. The young man nodded and went off.

"What have I done, Sir Charles? Why is everyone staring at me?" Sophie whispered, bewildered.

"Done? I do not know what you can be talking about, Miss Moore." He then called out, in a louder voice, "Arthur! Why are the musicians not playing? It is not even eleven o'clock. You young people cannot be tired already. Take your partners, everyone. Arthur, did you not say you had reserved this dance for Miss Moore?"

Arthur hesitated, and Sophie's gloved hand dangled conspicuously in the air for a moment. In that moment, which seemed to last an eternity, Sophie thought she must either run out of the room or die on the spot. She was still utterly in the dark as to what faux pas she had committed. But she knew every eye in the room was upon her, and she felt embarrassingly conspicuous in her puce-colored gown, since almost all of the other young ladies were garbed in demure white.

Then she saw a flash of scarlet approach her and a young man's voice say, "Pardon me for contradicting you, Sir Charles, but Miss Moore has promised me this dance."

The young officer led Sophie to a place in the line that was now beginning to form. Through the tears that clouded her eyes, she looked up and saw the face of Captain Banks, who had served in Jamaica for two years, with her father's regiment, and had returned to England a few months before Sophie's father died.

Captain Banks, who had come to the ball as a friend of some invited guests, was a gracious partner and he made a gallant effort to engage Sophie in conversation, speaking of mutual acquaintances, London's charms and other neutral topics. Sophie did her best to reply in kind, while being careful to keep her attention on the intricate steps of the dance so as not to embarrass her dance partner. But every time she saw Lady Jane and Miss Bryce-Joyce, who tittered whenever their eyes met, the feeling of shame and fluster returned. The two young ladies had somehow played a part in her public humiliation — and a knowing part, if their smirks were any indication.

When the music came to an end, Sophie thanked Captain Banks but declined his offer of refreshments. He bowed and disappeared into the crowd, and at last she could disappear too!

CHAPTER XII

HER FIRST THOUGHT WAS TO rush up to her room, where she could cry her heart out undisturbed. But a small group of ladies was coming down the stairs, after adjusting their toilette in the guest room that had been provided for that purpose and blocking her path. Sophie therefore darted into the one other room that had been her refuge, the library.

She flung open the window that led onto a small garden at the back of the house and breathed in the night air. She did not care if the air was damp and the night cold. Her one wish was to cool her flushed cheeks and the burning pain in her heart. Yet, she knew there was not enough air in the world to obscure the image of Arthur Wentworth as he had looked on the dance floor when he had refused to take her hand. That would be seared upon her heart for life.

She heard the door to the library open and she quickly wiped away her tears.

"Miss Moore? Here is your glass of punch." Henry Wentworth reached out his hand and offered the glass. "Though if you would rather punch me instead, do go ahead."

Sophie laughed, in spite of herself, but she did not leave her place by the window.

"Seriously, Miss Moore, we behaved abominably in the ballroom, so if you would like to throw this punch in my face or chase me around the room with a poker, I am at your service."

"If you truly wish to be of service, Mr. Wentworth, you will tell me what I did to offend."

"You did nothing, Miss Moore. The offense is all on our side."

"If you were a true friend, you would tell me."

Henry considered. Although they had known each other only a short while, their relationship had been marked by frankness from the first. He therefore put down the glass of punch and said, "It is your dress."

"My dress?" Sophie looked down at her costume. "How did I offend with my dress?"

"Oh, the dress is fine. Very elegant. It is just that the color ... You see, puce was my mother's favorite color. She always wore it, if not her dress then at least something that was the color — a shawl or parasol, well, you know the things you women pile on when you go out. After she died, it became a sort of rule in the family not to wear anything puce, out of respect for her memory and my father's feelings. You could not have known, of course. But when you appeared in the doorway, well, it was a shock. I still cannot understand why Lady Harrington did not warn you."

"She did not know about the dress."

"Well, that explains it. May I escort you back to the ballroom?"

Sophie shook her head.

"What about our dance? You did promise me one."

"Go back to your friends, Mr. Wentworth. I understand if you and ... and everyone in your family wish me in Jericho."

"I suppose every orphan feels a bit like Jericho's child at some time, but you are not in the way at all, Miss Moore. I know for a fact that my father has a sincere regard for you. And I do too."

Sophie was not sure if Henry had intentionally left out Arthur Wentworth from those who thought well of her, but she knew he was the only person in the ballroom who mattered to her. If she had his esteem, she had enough courage to face ten ballrooms filled with snickering Miss Bryce-Joneses and Lady Janes. But if he was angry at her blunder, or among those who would be laughing at her, she could not guarantee she would be able to maintain her composure under his disapproving gaze. It was therefore better to beat a retreat than suffer another humiliating defeat in public.

"Please, Mr. Wentworth, go back to the dance. I shall be fine."

"Not while you are in a brown study dark enough to match your gown." Henry walked over to the fireplace and removed the poker from its place. Offering it to Sophie, he said, "My mother always said it was never good to keep strong emotions bottled up inside. Give me a jab."

Again, Sophie found herself smiling, against her will. "It would be unfair. You are unarmed, sir."

Henry took up the cast iron shovel and assumed a fencing position. "Now we are evenly matched."

Sophie could not resist. She raised the poker and made her attack. For a few happy minutes the pair "fenced" their way around the room with their makeshift swords. At first, Henry played the gentleman and allowed Sophie to win a point. But after it dawned upon him that she actually knew something about swordsmanship, he began to fight back in earnest. He could not climb upon the furniture, since that would give him an unfair advantage; Sophie's long dress precluded her from hopping onto the library table or overturning chairs. But they both thoroughly enjoyed the thoroughly unorthodox fencing bout, until they both realized at the same moment that they were being watched by Sir Charles and Arthur, who were staring at them with unabashed surprise.

"Henry!" Sir Charles shouted, when he was finally able to give voice to his shocked sensibilities. "Have you gone mad, raising your hand to a young lady? Give me that shovel at once!"

"It is not what it seems, Father."

"Return to the ballroom and your guests. I will speak with you later."

Henry obeyed. After handing the shovel to Sir Charles, he bowed to Sophie and left the room.

Sir Charles approached Sophie, whose cheeks were still glowing from the vigorous exercise. "Miss Moore, I do not know what has gotten into everyone tonight. But if my son has done anything to insult your honor ..."

It was all Sophie could do not to laugh. "I assure you, Sir Charles, your son has acted like a perfect gentleman. He explained about my dress — and I am deeply sorry if my choice of color has caused you distress."

Sir Charles waved away any distress he may have felt with his hand. "It was a surprise. I will grant you that, Miss Moore. But my wife would have been very distressed by what happened tonight. She never wished to cause another person embarrassment, for any reason. So perhaps it is time to lay aside the custom. But do not feel obliged to protect Henry. I saw the way you were forced to fight off his advances. He shall pay for his behavior, Miss Moore. He shall pay!"

Sir Charles vigorously shook the shovel to demonstrate his intent. But his display was interrupted by the appearance of Miss Wentworth, who said, "Sir Charles, you have not spoken more than two words to Lady Carr all night. Everyone has noticed the slight."

Sir Charles looked momentarily befuddled, as he tried to sort out where his duties lay. Finally, he gave a nod to Sophie and thrust the shovel into Arthur's hands. "He shall pay!" And with those words he obediently followed his sister back to the ballroom and his guests.

Arthur waited until they were gone, and then he said, "You lied to me, Miss Moore."

Sophie looked puzzled. She could not think why he was laying this new offense at her door.

"That day you came out of the library and dropped your book. You told me you did not know how to fence."

There was something about his voice and the look in his eye that made Sophie shiver and grow warm, all at the same time. Somehow, she managed to return his smile. "As I recall, I parried your question with a feint."

Arthur put the shovel back in its stand. "Perhaps one day I shall have the privilege of engaging you in a match. Or are your affections reserved for my brother?"

Sophie stared, completely caught off guard. "I assure you, Mr. Wentworth, your brother's actions were strictly honorable—and so were mine."

Arthur came to her, until he was quite close, and looked down into her eyes. "A pity, for my brother."

Sophie felt the world go dark around her. Things were happening too quickly. She felt as though she were being hurtled from one end of eternity to another, with lightening-speed and with nothing to hold on to. All she could see was Arthur's eyes, which seemed to bore into her soul, binding her close, very close, to him.

They were now so close she could feel his breath upon her cheek. She closed her eyes. She sensed more than heard the words that he was saying.

"Perhaps I shall have better luck."

CHAPTER XIII

"OH! BEG YOUR PARDON I am sure!" Miss Bryce-Jones opened her fan with a sharp snap and raised it to her face, in pretense that she was not interested in the scene. Yet since the fan did not quite reach the level of her eyes, she eagerly took in everything.

Arthur had immediately backed away from Sophie, but it was too late. His intent to embrace the young woman had been all too clear. Her apparent willingness to be kissed was also clear.

Miss Bryce-Jones retreated from the doorway in triumph. In another minute, the incident would be making its whispered way about the ballroom. In another five, there would be no one who had not heard.

For once in his life, Arthur found himself in a situation he could neither control nor correct. He stammered a hurried "My apologies," and left Sophie alone in the room.

Sophie, too, was aware that her reputation had been compromised. Henry would have been able to make things right with Sir Charles; truth was on their side, since their relationship really was like sister and brother. But with Arthur Wentworth it was different. If he could insult her on the dance floor and she was still willing to let herself be kissed by him, she was lost. He could ask anything of her, and she would not have the strength to refuse. She must not remain in the Wentworth house another day.

She returned to her room, not seeing anyone and not caring. When she caught a glimpse of herself in the bedroom mirror, she began to furiously rip open the clasps of her dress, until she was free of the hated garment. She reached for her everyday dress and slipped it on. Then she set to work packing her things. If she did not receive word from Mr. Wentworth that evening — a proposal of marriage was the only thing that could repair the damage, and such a proposal was as likely as the sun changing places with the moon — in the morning, she would ask one of the servants to call for a carriage to take her to the coaching inn. If the weather was fine, she might be in Sevenoaks, the Kent village where Mr. and Mrs. Hemingway were staying, by dinner time.

Even with her new clothes, it did not take Sophie long to pack. She took her seat by the fire and waited.

"ARTHUR, COME HEAR THE NEWS," said Sir Charles, who had come in search of his elder son. The last of the guests had departed some time ago, Lady Carr was safely ensconced in her room for the night, and he had been in his study having a final glass of port when a messenger had appeared at the front door with a note from Lady Harrington.

"Not bad news, I hope," said Arthur, noticing the letter in his father's hand.

"On the contrary, I have not heard such a piece of good news in I do not know how many years."

By then they had returned to Sir Charles's study, and he closed the door behind them. "Old Hunks's turned dustman."

It took Arthur a full minute to decipher his father's cryptic words. "Hunks" of course referred to the Duke of Merton, a famous miser who had never wed and practically never left his vast estate in Surrey. Thus, the man was known more by reputation than any real familiarity with his person and tales about his eccentricities were exchanged and enlarged upon freely. "Turned dustman" was an informal way to say a person had passed away. Thus, putting two and two together Arthur came up with the conclusion that the Duke of Merton had passed away. What he still could not understand was why his father's eyes were gleaming so brightly.

"Is he a relation of ours? Do we inherit?"

"Not yet, Arthur, but we could — if you are willing."

"Me, sir?"

"Read this." Sir Charles thrust the letter he was holding into his son's hands.

Arthur recognized the handwriting of Lady Harrington at once. The hurriedly written note conveyed news Arthur already knew, the Duke's demise, and then reminded Sir Charles of who would inherit the title and estates: the Duke's nephew.

This of course means that dear Miss Appleby, the new Duke's only child, must now be addressed as Lady Anne (Lady Harrington wrote). *Appleby, of course, had more debts than hairs on his head before this, but now, Sir Charles, everything has changed. Overnight, he has become one of the richest men in England and he is certain to provide his only child with a dowry worthy of her new position in society. We must act at once — and Arthur, if you are reading this, as I am sure you will, you must not object. Such an opportunity does not come round more than a few times in a generation. Try not to be your usual imperious, stubborn self for a few weeks and make yourself agreeable to Lady Anne. Your loving niece and cousin, Mary*

Sir Charles began to rub his hands together with glee. "Merton! Charming place! The house is probably a bit rundown, but Appleby will fix that — or I should say 'his Grace.' La, what a funny thing that will be, calling Appleby 'your Grace.'"

Sir Charles then turned serious. "I owe you an apology, sir. All this time I thought you were being a young fool for not marrying Lady Jane. But now I see you were wise to wait. Lady Anne is worth ten of Lady Jane."

"I presume you mean in terms of fortune."

"Do not look down your long nose at me, sir. You yourself said a few days ago that all the young ladies were alike. You are entitled to your opinion. But all the same, eventually you will have to marry one of them, and if your heart is not otherwise engaged it may as well be Lady Anne. And she is a charming young lady. If for once in your life you exert yourself and make an effort, you might even grow to love her. Now, we must both write a letter of condolence to Appleby, I mean the Duke. And tomorrow you must go there and pay a call."

While Sir Charles went to the desk in his study to compose his missive, Arthur retired to the library. Although he had not considered an alliance with Lady Anne, due to her lack of a fortune before her stroke of good luck, Arthur found he was not entirely against the proposed marriage. Lady Anne was not a beauty of the first water, but she was pretty enough, endowed with pleasant rather than striking features.

True, the few times he had spoken to her she had had remarkably little to say. But she was young, only sixteen, which meant Arthur might succeed in molding her, so that one day her mind would be as elegant as her clothes.

And then there was the family seat at Merton. The property was entailed, of course. It would go to the nearest male relation after Appleby died, but that could be years away. In the meantime, Arthur could enjoy the old house, some of which dated back to Norman times, if he was not mistaken. He had only seen the property from a distance, once while visiting friends who lived nearby, but he had been enchanted by its possibilities. That was not to say he despised his own inheritance; the Wentworth country house was fine as far as country houses went, but it dated back to only Queen Anne, and so while it was relatively comfortable it lacked the depth of atmosphere that a truly old house had, a house like Merton. Under the right hands, Merton's great house and its grounds could be restored to its former glory, and he was confident he was up to the task. Perhaps this was the answer to his prayers—a chance to be enthusiastic about something, to feel a sense of accomplishment.

There was also the question of Lady Harrington's reputation. If Miss Thornhope had been correct, he owed it to Mary to at least try to stop the scandalous rumors from spreading even further. His marriage would put a temporary halt to the gossip-mongering, at any rate.

For a moment, his thoughts turned to Miss Moore, whose reputation had also been comprised due to his thoughtless action in the library. That had been a mistake on his part. If only he could have had his kiss without being seen. But the blame was not entirely his. She had acted in a most provocative way with his brother, gallivanting about the room in that reckless manner. What was he supposed to think? Still, it was a pity someone had seen them — and twice the pity that it had been a gossip peddler like Miss Bryce-Jones — because he liked Miss Moore. If she had been the one to have been revealed to be a duke's daughter, he would have pursued her hand with real pleasure.

Arthur set down his pen. It was true; he liked Miss Moore very much. Although he had thought her actions concerning the little chimney sweep absurdly quixotic, he admired her for having a warm heart and the courage to fight for what she wanted. He also admired the courage she had displayed in the ballroom, when she had taken her place in the dance, despite having been publicly humiliated just a few minutes earlier. And then there was the fire — the mischievous vitality — she had shown in the library, when she was fighting with Henry. Life with Miss Moore would be an adventure, a surprising and happy voyage through life.

But he was an elder son. With the privileges came responsibilities, even if those responsibilities were beginning to feel more and more like a noose tightening around his neck. The family must come first.

CHAPTER XIV

SIR CHARLES REREAD THE NOTE that had been placed by his seat at the breakfast table for perhaps the tenth time and shook his head in bewilderment. "Miss Moore fled to Sevenoaks, and without an abigail to accompany her."

"I told you it was a mistake to invite her to stay, Sir Charles, but you would not listen to me." Miss Wentworth buttered her toast with the satisfaction of one who has been proven right and relishes the victory.

"But we must do something. A young lady on her own ..."

"That sort of young 'lady' can take care of herself."

Henry threw down his napkin with disgust. "I will not allow you to insult Miss Moore in my presence."

"You would take her part," Dorothea replied with a sneer.

"Your aunt is right, Henry. What were you and Miss Moore doing in the library last night?"

"I only brought her a glass of punch, as you asked me to, Father."

"Served on a shovel?"

Henry sighed. "It was a jest. Miss Moore was in a brown study after the way Arthur insulted her ..."

"We will get to Arthur in a moment," said Sir Charles, shooting a glance in the direction of his eldest son.

"And so I told Miss Moore that if she wished to use me as her punching bag, to get out her anger at being insulted, I was at her service."

"Does Miss Moore box, too?" said Dorothea.

Henry ignored the comment. "I was only trying to cheer her up."

"I do not understand you young people," replied Sir Charles, shaking his head. "In my day, if a young man wanted to cheer up a lady he sent flowers."

"It was all perfectly harmless."

"I suppose I shall have to believe you, Henry. But the next time you are at a public ball and feel a need to cheer up a young lady, please find a more conventional way to do it. I do not know what Lady Carr will say if she hears about it."

Henry was not unduly concerned. Of all the members of the family, he got along the best with that lady precisely because she enjoyed hearing about all the scrapes he got into.

Sir Charles, having rebuked one son to his satisfaction, turned his attention to Arthur. Once again, his countenance became gloomy. "Your offense is much more serious, Arthur. I cannot think how we shall make amends."

"Nonsense, it was only a kiss," said Dorothea Wentworth. "I presume."

"Not even that, Aunt," replied Arthur, realizing for the first time how much he intensely disliked his Aunt Dorothea. "The incident has been blown entirely out of proportion."

"Still, what happened is not what matters," said Sir Charles. "It is what people say, and by now people are very likely saying you have given Miss Moore carte blanche and hidden her away someplace in town. I cannot like it. No, I cannot like it one bit. Neither will Lady Carr or Appleby. I mean, his Grace. Why did all this have to happen last night?"

"I refuse to see why you are making such a fuss," said Dorothea. "Pay her off with a sum of money, as is usually done."

"How would you know what is usually done, Aunt Dorothea?" asked Henry.

Miss Wentworth blushed furiously and nearly spilled her tea.

"But I do not see what Mr. Appleby has to do with Arthur and Miss Moore," said Henry.

"Didn't you hear? No, of course you didn't," said Sir Charles. "You had already gone up to bed when the message came. Appleby is now the Duke of Merton."

Henry looked astonished. "The Duke of Merton?!"

Their conversation was interrupted by the entrance of Lady Harrington, who was looking uncommonly flustered. She took a place in the center of the room, and announced in a low and trembling voice, "I have terrible news."

"If it is about Miss Moore's departure, we already know," said Sir Charles.

"Miss Moore? It is about Lady Anne that I have come. Oh, Arthur, how could you have done this?"

Arthur raised an eyebrow.

"What on earth has he done now?" asked Sir Charles, raising both of his eyebrows for good measure.

"I paid Lady Anne a call early this morning," said Lady Harrington. "She was not receiving visitors and so I left her a little note, just hinting that Arthur wished to pay his respects later in the day, and you will not believe what she wrote back." Lady Harrington removed the missive from her pineapple-shaped reticule. "She writes that she cannot possibly consider an alliance with Arthur, and so there is no need for him to call."

There was a gloomy silence for several minutes. Then Sir Charles roused himself and said, "She'll change her mind. This is just hysterics. After all, it was just a kiss. Mary, you must tell everyone Arthur has not offered carte blanche to anyone. Say that you have it on my authority that Miss Moore was ... was ..."

"Called away suddenly to be by the bedside of a dying aunt?" offered Lady Harrington.

"Excellent." Sir Charles then turned to his son. "Tomorrow, Arthur, you must pay Lady Anne a morning call. And today, send her flowers!"

Lady Harrington poured out a cup of tea. Now that her plan to marry off Arthur to Lady Anne had been salvaged, she had returned to her usual good spirits. "I shall also do my part. I shall suggest a drive in the park in my carriage this afternoon. You, Arthur, must be there, too, though I cannot decide if you should be driving your curricle or riding your horse, you always look so elegant no matter what you do. But just doff your hat. Do not try to speak to her. I shall do that for you."

Arthur studied her for a few moments. Then he said, "Have you no interest in what has become of Miss Moore?"

"Should I?"

"She has left London and gone to Sevenoaks."

Lady Harrington shrugged. "It is probably just as well. Perhaps she will attract the eye of one of my husband's tenant farmers. But that reminds me, I have received an excellent suggestion for a new headmistress from Lady Prudence. You were right not to offer the position to Miss Moore. She would not have suited our needs at all."

Arthur turned away. This was not the first time he had seen Lady Harrington take up people and projects only to throw them away when they no longer amused her. In the past, he had always made excuses for her behavior. How could a goddess be expected to behave like an ordinary mortal? This morning, though, he could not ignore the truth, difficult as it was to shatter the idol he had so lovingly created with the ardor of youth. Lady Harrington had beauty and wit and vivacity, but he now saw she was deficient in one important area, as were so many people in his circle: she had no heart.

SOPHIE SAT IN THE CORNER of the coach, hoping no one would speak to her. She was aware that no respectable young woman of the gentry would travel alone, although a governess traveling to a new position might. She therefore tried to appear stern and strong, both unapproachable and irreproachable. Apparently her ruse was successful, since no one said a word to her during the journey.

When she and her trunk and bandbox were deposited at the White Hart, a large coaching inn that served Sevenoaks, she was unsure what to do next. There had not been time to warn Mr. and Mrs. Hemingway of her arrival, and for an anxious moment she fretted that the cottage where they were staying might not be in the village after all.

Fortunately, a man with a cart and a horse, whose business it was to greet the coaches that rumbled into the village, approached her and asked if he could be of service. He recognized the name Hemingway and assured Sophie that she would be at their cottage in less than half an hour. After her trunk was loaded onto the cart, Sophie clambered onto the seat beside the driver. It was a far cry from the elegance of Lady Harrington's carriage, but Sophie did not care. Her one thought was that soon she would see the face of her old friend, and when the cart stopped in front of the cottage and a curious Mrs. Hemingway appeared at the front door, Sophie flew down from her perch and flung herself into the surprised but open arms of Mrs. Hemingway.

"There, there child," said Mrs. Hemingway, gently leading inside Sophie, who was sobbing uncontrollably. "You sit by the fire and rest yourself, while I make you a nice cup of tea."

Mrs. Hemingway directed the driver to take Sophie's trunk upstairs, where there was an empty bedroom, and then she paid him his wages. "Poor thing, she has lost her father," she whispered to the man, who gave her an understanding nod and then departed. Mrs. Hemingway knew that people talked as much in villages as they did in town, and so it was better to have Sophie's odd behavior explained by grief than something more compromising.

"Whatever it is, you can tell me in the morning," said Mrs. Hemingway, when she returned to the front room of the cottage. "Tonight, you need a good meal and a rest."

"I ... I will not be in the way, will I?" asked Sophie. "Your sister will not mind that I have come?"

"She is visiting some relatives of her late husband for a few weeks, so we shall be quite alone. Mr. Hemingway will join us later, of course. But he has found work in the great house, helping to train a new horse. It is Lord Harrington's place — very grand from what I hear, but I have yet to see milord or milady. They are in London. Why, Sophie, whatever is wrong with you, child? You look white as a ghost. Are you ill?"

Sophie shook her head.

It was then the turn of Mrs. Hemingway to turn pale. "Did anything happen in London, Sophie? Did you ... have you ...?"

Sophie shook her head a second time. "Oh, Mrs. Hemingway," she said, as the tears once again flowed from her eyes, "I am in love."

Mrs. Hemingway sighed with relief. But a moment later her anxiety returned. A confession of love could have been written in a letter. If Sophie had felt compelled to leave the Wentworth house, there had to be more to the story. Yet she did not rush Sophie. Instead, she let the girl talk at her own pace, allowing time for fresh bursts of tears and cups of tea, until she had heard the tale in its entirety.

"You did the right thing, Sophie," she said, patting the girl's arm. "You could not have stayed in that house another night and preserved your reputation. I am only sorry Mr. Wentworth has won your heart. He does not deserve it."

THE NEXT MORNING SOPHIE AWOKE to blue skies and the sound of birds chirping in the garden. When she went down to the front room, Mr. and Mrs. Hemingway were seated at the breakfast table, and they both greeted her with cheerful smiles. The usual inquiries were made as to how Sophie had passed the night, and she reassured them she had slept well. They were all careful not to mention the reason why Sophie had come to Kent.

After breakfast, Mrs. Hemingway suggested a walk and Sophie agreed. Mrs. Hemingway chose a path that took them through pleasant green fields, which culminated in a long row of ancient Sweet Chestnut trees. Sophie could feel her spirits revive, and she commented as much to her friend.

"I always say a long walk in the country does more good than an ocean of hartshorn," replied Mrs. Hemingway. "In a few months you hopefully will have forgotten all about that young man."

"Will your sister allow me to stay in her home for so long?"

"You must not worry about that. I am certain she will love you as much I do."

Mrs. Hemingway began to gather some chestnut leaves, which she said were good for curing aches and pains of the muscles and joints. Sophie helped her, and the exercise did her good. Employed thus, with Mrs. Hemingway as her companion, reminded

Sophie of happier days back in Jamaica, where they had made similar foraging excursions.

However, when they returned to the cottage they saw there was a letter waiting for Sophie, and the two women eyed it with misgiving.

"You may take it upstairs to your room, if you like," said Mrs. Hemingway.

"I have no wish to keep secrets from you," Sophie replied.

The two sat down at the table and Sophie tore open the seal. As she unfolded the letter, a bank note fell down upon the table. They let it remain there, while Sophie read the letter out loud. It was from Sir Charles, expressing his regret about the misunderstanding that had occurred under his roof and begging her forgiveness for any unintended slight she might have incurred. He concluded by saying he would be pleased if Miss Moore would make use of the enclosed sum however she saw fit.

"It is a kind letter, is it not?" she said to Mrs. Hemingway. "Sir Charles is a kind man."

"It is fine, as far as it goes."

"He does not ask me to come back, of course, or ask me to call when I am next in London, but I do not expect that. I understand it is best if the connection is severed, forever."

Sophie's lips began to tremble.

"One day your heart will agree," Mrs. Hemingway reassured her.

"What shall I do about the money?" Sophie glanced at the sum. It was very generous. "I could set up a music school. Not in London, but somewhere else. Yet, I do not wish to accept it. Am I being selfish if I refuse this gift?"

"How so?"

"Well, I shall have to take advantage of your hospitality that much longer, until I find a position."

"Do not worry your head about that, Sophie. I have already said you may stay here as long as you like."

Sophie wrote her letter and enclosed the bank note. When the letter had been handed over to the postman, she said to Mrs. Hemingway, "Now it is truly over. I shall not hear from them again."

CHAPTER XV

SOPHIE'S CONNECTION TO THE WENTWORTH family turned out to be not so easily severed. The next day she was very surprised to see a carriage pull up in front of the cottage — and see Henry hand down Miss Appleby (now Lady Anne). When she came outside to greet the visitors, Henry rushed toward her, with Lady Anne in tow.

"May we speak inside?" Henry said in a low voice and without preamble.

Sophie showed the two into the sitting room. Mrs. Hemingway had gone to the village, and so she explained that they were quite alone.

"Miss Moore, I do not know what makes me so bold, considering I have not had the honor of being acquainted with you for very long. But in that short time, I hope ..."

"Mr. Wentworth, there is no need to play the swain with me. State your request, although I think I can guess what it is."

Sophie glanced over at Lady Anne, who was looking both very much in love and frightened to death.

"We have eloped," said Henry, clasping Lady Anne's hand a little tighter. "We must reach Gretna Green without being discovered."

Sophie's knowledge of England was hazy, yet she did know that Kent was not the shortest route to Scotland. She also knew that to harbor an eloping couple was no simple thing, especially when one half of the runaway couple was the son of the gentleman who had lately offered her a home and protection.

Henry saw her perplexed look. "You must not think this a rash decision on our part. Miss Appleby, I mean Lady Anne, and I have intended to elope for a very long time. Before her father became the Duke of Merton and inherited the estate ..."

Sophie looked in wonder at the young lady, who said, "We only received the news two nights ago that my great-uncle had passed away. Before that, my father and mother and I were practically paupers."

"That is why my father would not agree to the match," Henry continued. "He insisted that since I was a younger son and would not inherit very much, I had to marry for money. I pretended to go along, but Miss Appleby and I decided that once she reached the age of sixteen and I reached my twenty-first birthday and would inherit the little money I was entitled to, we would elope."

Sophie was trying to follow the story as best she could, but she was still puzzled. "If Lady Anne is now an heiress, why then do you need to elope? Surely, Sir Charles cannot object to your marrying now."

"It is my father who now objects," said Lady Anne. "Now that he is a duke and I am a duke's daughter, he wishes to marry me off to duke, or at least an earl. But I could not possibly marry anyone else," she said, turning to Henry. "Mr. Wentworth is the only man I have ever cared for. I could never love anyone else."

The two young lovers gazed into each other's eyes, and Sophie was certain their love was sincere.

Here was a love that was not dependent upon wealth or title, and she wished she could help them.

"Why, though, have you come to Sevenoaks?" she asked Henry.

"When Anne's father discovers she has fled, he is sure to raise the alarum. Everyone will rightly guess that our intention is to flee to Gretna Green, and they will make every effort to overtake us. But if Miss Appleby could stay with you for a few days, while I also find shelter nearby, we could fool them by taking a different route and foil their plans to stop us."

The two looked hopefully at Sophie, who was looking undecided. She could not forget her debt to Sir Charles, no matter how much she wanted to help them, and she said so.

"If that is what is preventing you from helping us, Miss Moore, you may be assured that now that Miss Appleby is a duke's daughter and an heiress, my father will not object at all to the marriage. Indeed, he will be very pleased."

Sophie had to admit this was very likely true. There was one last objection that had to be resolved, however. The cottage was not hers. She could not offer refuge to Lady Anne without first asking permission from Mrs. Hemingway.

Fortunately, that woman appeared at that moment and the lovers' plight was explained to her. Henry's entreaties did not fall on deaf ears. She agreed to harbor Lady Anne for a few days, on one condition — that Henry would do nothing to further compromise the young lady's reputation, or the good name of anyone living in the cottage. Henry of course agreed.

"You shall have to share a room with Miss Moore," said Mrs. Hemingway.

"I should like that," replied Lady Anne. "Mr. Wentworth has told me so much about you, Miss Moore. In the carriage he could barely speak of anything else."

A small trunk belonging to Lady Anne was brought inside, and the two young lovers made their tearful goodbyes. Sophie could not help but compare her own hasty flight with that of Lady Anne — and the memory made her recall her last night in London, when she had waited up all night in vain for a note, even one word, from Arthur Wentworth.

She also could not help but feel a twinge of envy for Lady Anne's good fortune. Henry Wentworth might lack cold cash, but he had a warm, affectionate heart, and Sophie had no doubt but that he would make his chosen bride very happy.

SIR CHARLES WAS AT HIS club when the new Duke of Merton came rushing into the room, all in a rage. It took several minutes to decipher what was at the bottom of the duke's bout of uncontrolled fury, but when Sir Charles did finally understand he found it hard to conceal his delight.

"Henry? My son has eloped with your daughter?"

"Do you pretend you do not know, sir?"

"Of course, I do not know. I wanted Arthur to marry your daughter."

His Grace stopped to consider. Although his first thought upon assuming the title had been to make a brilliant match for his daughter, he knew dukes were expensive and often in a great deal of debt. It therefore might be better to marry off his only daughter to Arthur Wentworth, who not only was heir to a substantial fortune but had the prudence to preserve it.

"Then you will help me stop the pair?"

"You will agree to Lady Anne marrying my son Arthur?"

"I agree, only we must stop them before they reach Gretna Green."

"I am at your service ... your Grace!"

CHAPTER XVI

LEST IT BE THOUGHT THAT Sir Charles was heartless in his exchanging of one brother for another, he was not being heartless at all — only devious. He was as surprised as the duke to discover that Henry and Lady Anne cared for one another. But if it was true, and it appeared to be very true, then Sir Charles knew that Arthur would never consent to marry the lady. Arthur was much too proud to marry his younger brother's castoff lover. Therefore, if Sir Charles wished to have a duke's daughter in the family, the marriage between Henry and Lady Anne must happen. The only question was how to do it respectably, and not over the anvil at Gretna Green, which was not respectable at all.

This was the question that he posed to Arthur and Lady Harrington back at his home — for of course that lady had been invited to the important family meeting.

If Arthur was perturbed to learn that Lady Anne preferred Henry to him, he did not show it. Even within the intimate family circle, he remained the perfect English gentleman — unruffled by whatever life might throw at him. Inwardly, however, he was in such turmoil that he could scarcely keep his mind on the conversation going on between his father and Lady Harrington. All he could think about was his younger brother, how Henry had surpassed him completely. By daring everything in a bid for happiness, Henry had shown his mettle. And Arthur wondered whether he would have the courage to do the same.

"What do you think, Arthur? Will Mary's scheme work?"

"His mind is a million miles away," said Lady Harrington. "What devious plot have you concocted in your masculine mind, Arthur? I am sure it will excel anything that a weak woman could think of."

"I think yours is an excellent plan, Mary," said Sir Charles. "While the Duke of Merton takes his route to Scotland, wasting time by stopping at inns and turnpikes to see if the eloping couple has passed that way, we will drive straight to Gretna Green with all the speed we can muster. We will catch Henry and Lady Anne before they exchange vows over the anvil and explain the situation. Then, when his Grace finally arrives we will give him the ultimatum — either he agrees to a proper church wedding, or the blacksmith will do the honors."

Sir Charles went off to make the preparations. In addition to readying the horses and the carriage, they would need an ample supply of food and wine, since if they would be traveling, they might as well travel in comfort. He also needed to pack a few changes of linen and other clothing for the long journey. There was also Lady Carr to consider — although that lady turned out to be less perturbed by the news of the elopement than he had expected. Indeed, she agreed to remain in the house with only Miss Wentworth as company, until the eloping couple was brought back to London, which Sir Charles thought was remarkably gracious and understanding of her.

Since Arthur also needed to pack a few things for the journey, he made his excuses and goodbyes to Lady Harrington.

"I envy you gentlemen and your adventures," replied Lady Harrington, rising from her seat. "How I wish I could come with you."

"I assure you the journey will be exceedingly long, tiresome and boring."

"It will give you time to think, though."

"Should I use the time to think about anything in particular?"

Lady Harrington gave him one of her dazzling smiles. "You must think of a way to return to the good graces of Lady Jane. You must make some public act of contrition so she can forgive you."

"Forgive me?"

"Yes, forgive you for your lapse with Miss Moore. We know the kiss meant nothing, but a young lady does like to see her lover grovel and beg for forgiveness before the wedding — since we all know it will never happen afterward."

"And what makes you think I will forgive her?"

"Forgive her? For what?"

"She played a mean trick on Miss Moore, advising her to wear puce."

"People say you are deep, Arthur, but I think you are just intentionally exasperating. What on earth does the color of Miss Moore's dress have to do with your marrying Lady Jane?"

"I am not going to marry Lady Jane."

"I cannot think why you prefer Miss Bryce-Jones to an Earl's daughter."

"That is because I do not."

"Then who do you intend to marry, if I may ask?"

Arthur hesitated. Then he thought of Henry, who at that moment was very likely racing headlong toward his happiness. "I intend to marry Miss Moore, if she will have me."

Lady Harrington opened her eyes wide, and then she collapsed into a peal of laughter. "For a moment I thought you were serious, Arthur."

"And what if I am?"

"You cannot be. Oh, I will admit Miss Moore has her charms. But you could never be happy with someone who was not your equal. You know that."

"For once, we are in agreement. Fortunately, Miss Moore is not my equal. I believe she is my superior when it comes to many things, the sorts of things that matter in a marriage."

"Such as?"

"The ability to care deeply about another person."

Lady Harrington rolled her eyes. "My husband will cut you completely if you marry a nobody. So will Lady Carr."

"Two excellent reasons for paying my addresses to Miss Moore at once."

Lady Harrington took out her jewel-encrusted snuff box and took a pinch of snuff while she considered the matter. She offered the box to Arthur, but he declined. After putting the box back in her reticule, she said, "You are serious, aren't you?"

Arthur nodded.

"Well, this is a surprise. When do you intend to ask Miss Moore for her hand?"

In truth, an hour before this Arthur had not known he was going to do anything of the kind, and so he hesitated again, before saying, "When we get back from Scotland. Or perhaps I shall stop off at Sevenoaks on the way home."

"Sevenoaks? Ah, I had forgotten Miss Moore was staying there."

Lady Harrington allowed Arthur to escort her to the door. Before she left, though, she looked up at him and said, "You are not saying this just to exasperate me, are you? Do you truly love Miss Moore?"

"Yes, I do."

"Then I wish you success with your suit."

"Even though Miss Moore is not the daughter of a Duke or an Earl?"

Lady Harrington smiled and gave Arthur her hand. "When it comes to your happiness, Arthur, there is nothing I would not do."

CHAPTER XVII

WHEN LADY HARRINGTON WAS OCCUPIED with one of her schemes, she thought nothing of rising at dawn, or at least at nine o'clock, as she did the following morning. Her carriage was waiting for her after breakfast, and since the road to Kent was a good one — and since she knew that Arthur and Sir Charles were on their way to Scotland — she could sit back and enjoy the journey.

Her grand carriage caused considerable interest when it rolled into Sevenoaks, and even more talk after her coachman inquired for the cottage where the Hemingways were staying and drove off in that direction.

Sophie was in the garden, cutting some flowers when she first heard the rumble of the wheels. Her heart skipped a beat, as it always did when a carriage passed by. Despite her insistence that Henry keep his distance from the cottage, so as not to give the plot away, he had acted as a true lover, unable to be parted from his love for more than a few hours. Sophie was therefore worried that someone from the village had recognized one or both of the pair and sent word back to London. To her surprise, though, it was not the Duke or Sir Charles who descended from the carriage.

Instead, it was Lady Harrington, and her face was wreathed with smiles when she saw Sophie. "How well you look, Miss Moore!" she exclaimed with delight. "The country air agrees with you, I see."

As it was a sunny day, Lady Harrington suggested they sit outside — there was a stone bench at the far end of the garden — and have a comfortable coze. "No tea for me," she said, waving aside the offer, while arranging her traveling costume, a dream of heavenly sky blue trimmed with fur. "I must be off in a quarter of an hour, and I would much rather spend the time hearing all about you."

Sophie did not know what to say. She certainly could not chat about the eloping lovers. As for herself, although she always found a way to keep occupied, either by helping Mrs. Hemingway in the house or taking long walks, she could not imagine this would interest Lady Harrington.

Fortunately, Lady Harrington filled the pause with her own cheerful chatter for several minutes. Then she said, with a knowing look on her face, "I do not suppose you have yet heard the news. Henry Wentworth has eloped."

"With who?" asked Sophie, hoping she had succeeded in looking genuinely surprised.

"Lady Anne, the daughter of the Duke of Merton."

"How extraordinary."

"It seems Lady Anne won his heart ages ago," said Lady Harrington with a smile. "But that is not my only news. It seems that a very lucky lady has won the heart of Arthur Wentworth. Can you guess who that lady is?"

Sophie looked down at the flowers that were sitting in her lap. What had seemed to be such a pretty bouquet just a few minutes earlier now presented a truer picture; cut from their source of vitality, they were just dead things. Already, their colors were fading.

She was fairly certain of what was coming, the announcement that Mr. Wentworth was going to marry either Lady Jane or Miss Bryce-Jones. She knew she should not care, yet she wished she was going to hear the news in another way, in a letter she could read in the privacy of her room, for example. Instead, she listlessly pulled off a few of the petals. But instead of silently thinking "he loves me, he loves me not," her mind was perversely whispering: Lady Jane, Miss Bryce-Jones. Lady Jane, Miss Bryce-Jones.

Lady Harrington let Miss Moore sit in suspense for several minutes, while she observed every change of color, every movement, in that young lady's face. When she was convinced Sophie returned Arthur Wentworth's feelings, she laid her hand on Sophie's arm. "It is you, Miss Moore. Mr. Wentworth is in love with you."

Sophie looked up, too astonished to speak.

"I do not know how you managed to do it, but you have cast a spell over him and he absolutely refuses to consider anyone else. Are you pleased, Miss Moore? Are you happy? Shall I tell Mr. Wentworth that you would consent to marry him, if he asks?"

Sophie was still too surprised to say a word. The garden, the bench they were sitting on — in an instant none of it felt real. Instead, she was enwrapped in a whirl of conflicting emotions that made her feel quite dizzy. Astonishment, doubt, giddy happiness — she felt she could not contain it all, that she must either burst or float away. The only thing that kept her connected to everyday life was the pressure of Lady Harrington's hand on her arm.

"You are happy. I can see it in your face," said Lady Harrington, tightening her grasp. "But Miss Moore, think carefully before you give me your answer. You come from a very different circle, you know, and you would not be accepted by all of Mr. Wentworth's acquaintances. I do not hold against you the fact that you have neither wealth nor title. I think such snobbery is absurd. But I know the nobility, and how they behave. You are a woman of great sensitivity and sensibility. You will not enjoy being snubbed."

Thoughts flitted quickly in Sophie's brain. She could see there was some truth in what Lady Harrington was saying, and yet ... "If Mr. Wentworth and I are happy, what would it matter?"

"Friends can be replaced, it is true, but what about family? Sir Charles will never forgive Arthur for marrying you. He has his heart set on Arthur making a brilliant match, one that will bring credit to the family, and not shame. It hurts me to say it, but I feel it is my duty to prepare you for the road that will lie ahead of you."

"Surely, Sir Charles will not remain angry forever. He is too generous and kind. When he sees that Mr. Wentworth and I are truly in love ..."

"But will he, Miss Moore? I do not like this part I must play — if you had a mother, someone who truly had your interests at heart, I would not do it — but you are so young. You do not know about life, about what often happens a year or two after a man and a woman marry for love. That love, Miss Moore, often does not last. A man grows bored very quickly, and when he realizes he has made a terrible mistake, that he has cut himself off from his family and friends because of a moment of folly, he begins to despise the woman he has married. When that happens, a man can seek some balm for his misery outside the home. But a woman, Sophie — may I call you Sophie, dear?"

Sophie nodded her head. As she did, a teardrop fell from her eye.

"I know my first loyalty should be to Arthur, since he is my cousin. But you are a woman, like I am, and there are times when a woman's loyalty must be to another one of her sex. I would not see you hurt for the world, Sophie, and you will be hurt, should you agree to marry Mr. Wentworth. I know him so much better than you, my dear."

Sophie could not deny the truth of Lady Harrington's words. How could she compare her own brief knowledge of the man with someone who had known him all her life? Yet, she knew that, irrational as it might seem to others, Arthur Wentworth was the only man she would ever love. If he wished to marry her, she could not give up her one chance for happiness.

"Lady Harrington, I am grateful to you for coming here, for speaking to me so frankly. But I must take my chances and pray that our marriage will be one of those that are happy."

"Then you intend to accept Mr. Wentworth's offer, when he proposes?"

"Yes, I do."

Lady Harrington removed her hand from Sophie's arm and opened her reticule. She took out a folded note and opened it. "Do you recognize this, Miss Moore? Let me show it to you. It is your promise to me to repay a favor. You signed your name to it that day in the carriage. Remember?"

Sophie stared down at the handwriting. She could not deny it was hers.

"Today is the day I claim payment of the debt you owe me. I ask that you give up Mr. Wentworth. When he asks you to marry him, you must decline."

Sophie stared at Lady Harrington, unable to comprehend. "I do not understand. That day ... We were laughing ... How can you ask me to do this?"

"You stipulated no conditions. I can ask what I please."

"But ..."

"This is a debt of honor, Miss Moore. I think you know what that means."

Sophie did. She had grown up in a world where a debt of honor was sacred. Her father would have gone without wine for a year, rather than renege on a debt that he owed to a fellow soldier. If she now went back on her word, not only would she lose her own self-respect, but she would sully the good name of her father.

The tears were welling up in Sophie's eyes and she did not want Lady Harrington to see them. Yet, she knew that lady would not leave until she received an answer. For some reason which she did not completely understand, Lady Harrington was determined, and Sophie could not see a way to successfully fight her. All the most powerful weapons in the arsenal were on that lady's side.

Sophie took a deep breath. "I give you my word, Lady Harrington."

"I want to hear you say it. I want *you* to hear yourself say it."

By then the tears were falling down Sophie's face and she did not care who saw them. She was utterly defeated.

"I will not marry Mr. Wentworth."

"Someday you will thank me, Miss Moore," said Lady Harrington, resuming her light-hearted manner.

After shaking off a few stray leaves that had fallen upon her pelisse, she returned to her carriage. The coachman snapped his whip and the horses set the carriage in motion. Lady Harrington appeared at the window and waved her hand, as though she and Sophie had just enjoyed a delightful visit. "Goodbye."

Lady Anne, who had been watching the scene from the window with growing horror, rushed to the garden bench and flung her arm about Sophie's waist.

"You are so brave, Miss Moore. I admire you so much. I could never have done what you have just done. I could never have given up Henry, not for anything in the world."

Lady Anne babbled on, trying to comfort Sophie. But Sophie did not really hear her. All she could hear was the echo of her own words: *I will not marry Mr. Wentworth.*

CHAPTER XVIII

THE NEXT MORNING HENRY AND Lady Anne set off for Gretna Green. Mrs. Hemingway made sure their carriage was stocked with many good provisions, since the fewer inns the young couple stopped at the better.

"This will be the true test to see if they are suited or not," said Mrs. Hemingway, after the carriage had disappeared into the early morning mist. "If they can survive five or six days on the road without coming to blows, they should be able to face anything together."

Mrs. Hemingway need not have worried. The eloping couple spent most of the journey staring into each other's eyes, oblivious to the ruts in the road, the dust and the other many little inconveniences. Even the variable comforts of the inns where they spent the night — in separate rooms, of course — did not damper their pleasure. It was enough that they were together, that soon they would be married, that they had their whole lives ahead of them, and that great happiness was sure to be their lot.

The journey did have its anxious moments. Once, when they were changing horses, Lady Anne spied her father pacing up and down in front of the coaching inn. Fortunately, there was an available team of horses for them to hire and the young hostler who did the exchange was faster than lightening.

Henry and Lady Anne were off again almost before the Duke realized a carriage had come and gone.

When the Duke of Merton did realize, he rushed up to the young man and plied him with questions. But the hostler pretended he had not noticed who was in the carriage; his eye had been on the horses, since that was his job. And, of course, he did not mention the shiny coin that Henry had given him, to purchase his silence.

"I hope your father is on his way back to London," said Henry. "He cannot be on his way to Scotland, if he left immediately after discovering your note."

"Do you think he will be terribly angry at us for what we have done?" asked Lady Anne. An anxious look was momentarily marring her youthful beauty. "I should never forgive myself if he should become ill from worry, or grief."

Henry gave her hand a reassuring squeeze. "No one could ever be angry at you for long, my love. When he sees how happy you are — and I will make you happy, I promise — he will relent and give us his blessing."

Lady Anne was reassured by this answer. She nestled closer to Henry, certain the happy picture he had just painted would prove to be a true likeness.

ARTHUR STRETCHED HIS WEARY LIMBS, oblivious to the admiring stares of the stable hands who had assembled in the coaching inn's courtyard. His caped greatcoat was not spotless — he had been on the road for too many hours to not collect some of that road's dust — but the quality of the cloth and cut of the coat, as well as the easy elegance with which he wore it, alerted the rustic workers that a gentleman from London was in their presence.

Arthur had not expected to arrive at this inn on horseback, but the journey had taken an unexpected turn the previous day, when Sir Charles ate a dubious piece of fish and shortly afterward suffered the consequences. The wretched assault on his digestion had also set off an old heart ailment, and the gentleman was in no state to travel further.

"You must go on alone, Arthur," Sir Charles had said from his bed. "Henry and Lady Anne cannot reach Gretna Green before us."

Arthur did not like to leave his father alone in a coaching inn, especially when Sir Charles was ill. But after he saw that the worst of the crisis had passed and that Sir Charles only needed a day of rest and then he would be restored to health, Arthur agreed to hire a horse and travel onward in the morning. The carriage would remain at the service of Sir Charles.

Thus, Arthur found himself alone at an inn in northern England, waiting until a fresh horse could be provided. As the wait was proving to be longer than he had hoped, he allowed the innkeeper to convince him to go inside and have some refreshments.

The main room smelled of smoke and ale and meat roasting on the fire. The half-timbered ceiling was sagging in the middle, but none of the motley crew gathered in the room seemed to mind. Seated at a large table in the center of the room was a group of commercial travelers, who were finishing the last of what looked to be a substantial dinner. Their natural joviality, a prerequisite of the profession, was being liberally enhanced by some of the inn's strong brew.

Closer to the fire sat two vicars, who were either traveling together or had sought out each other's more sedate company, since at that moment they sat huddled together in earnest conversation. A few solitary men, from their looks the sort who purchased the outside seats on the mail coaches whether the weather was rainy or fine, sat on the bench that lined the far end of the room, tankards in their hands and woebegone looks in their eyes.

There were no people of Arthur's circle in the public dining room, since they would have engaged a private sitting room, especially if ladies were part of the traveling party. But since Arthur did not intend to stay long, or to order a full dinner — cold meat and bread would do — he did not bother to reserve a private sitting room for himself. He espied a small, quiet table where he could eat his meal, noticed only by the portrait of somebody's grandfather, which hung lopsided on the plastered wall opposite him. However, when he saw George Somerton enter the room with some request for the innkeeper and his friend recognized him, Arthur accepted the invitation to join Somerton in his private room.

"I just saw your brother," said Somerton, pouring out a glass of wine for Arthur. "I suppose you are here for the same reason as I am — going to the boxing match. Who do you plan to bet on? I've placed my money on Ned Painter. Were you at the match last August? That was something a person won't be likely to forget. I placed my bet on Coyne, to my regret. But I don't intend to make that mistake again."

When there was finally a pause in the monologue, Arthur inquired whether Somerton had indeed seen Henry in the inn or had been speaking in a general way.

"It was here, all right. If I am not mistaken there was a young lady with him." Somerton gave Arthur a wink.

"I had better go see what he is up to," said Arthur. It would not do for Somerton to suspect the truth, not if they were to succeed in keeping the elopement a secret.

The innkeeper was in the main room, busy serving his guests, when Arthur came to find him. Arthur managed to get the man to follow him back to the corridor that led to the private rooms. "There is a newly married couple here. Please direct me to their sitting room."

The innkeeper made a pretense of thinking deeply — Henry had given him the customary coin to buy his silence — and then shook his head with regret. "I believe you are mistaken, sir."

"The young lady is the only daughter of the Duke of Merton. If she is here, I advise you to tell me at once. Otherwise ..."

Arthur let the innkeeper imagine for himself what terrible punishment would befall him if he was caught harboring a Duke's runaway daughter. Apparently, the man had a first-rate imagination, since he immediately showed Arthur to the private sitting room where the young couple were sharing a meal.

Henry jumped up from his seat when he saw Arthur standing in the doorway. Lady Anne opened her mouth to let out a scream, but wisely clamped her lips shut before the sound came out. Arthur's estimation of her rose considerably.

At first, no one knew what to say, and so they just stared. When the silence began to verge on the ludicrous, Arthur said, "May I sit down, Lady Anne?"

Lady Anne nodded her assent, and Henry retook his seat.

"We shall not be separated," said Henry, regaining some of his courage now that the first moment of surprise had passed.

"Then you have not yet been to Gretna Green?"

"No, but, Arthur, you do not really intend to stop us, do you?"

"Of course, I do."

"Lady Anne will not marry you, will you, my love?" Henry looked in the young lady's direction and she rewarded with him a courageous smile, although her lips were trembling.

"I am sorry, Mr. Wentworth," she said to Arthur.

"I have no intention of marrying your beloved — no insult intended, ma'am — but you must not get married at Gretna Green. Our father has agreed to your marriage. There is reason to believe the Duke of Merton will also give his assent, after the necessary financial arrangements are made."

"Have you forgotten that the bulk of the family fortune goes to you?"

"Not all of the property is entailed, Henry. There are also some jewels we can sell. You will not have to arrive at the altar empty-handed, provided of course you exchange your marriage vows at an altar."

Henry jumped up and shook his brother by the hand. "I do not know what to say, except that this is very handsome of you, Arthur. I had no idea you could be so understanding, and so generous."

Arthur did not say what he was thinking, that if Henry had not eloped it probably would not have occurred to Arthur to part with even a small portion of his fortune. Yet, much had changed during the past several weeks, and now his one thought was to conclude the business with Henry and Lady Anne, so that he could begin to pursue his own happiness.

"However, you do not need to part with any of your fortune. After I explained my predicament to Lady Carr, we played a game of piquet and she allowed me to win a considerable sum of money. A small fortune, really. She only asked that I tell her all about the adventure after Lady Anne and I return from Scotland."

Arthur was amazed at this turn of events, but then he considered that Henry had always been a favorite with Lady Carr. That lady was very likely already making plans for Henry and Lady Anne to live near her, so she could play three-handed whist with them every evening.

However, they also had arrangements to make. Word had to be sent to Sir Charles and the Duke of Merton, who were both still traveling northward. Fortunately, they had made plans beforehand to leave word of their progress at certain changing stations along the way, and this coaching inn was one of them. Therefore, they need only wait until their respective fathers arrived.

Arthur did not relish having to play the role of chaperon, but he had no choice. He could not risk having the young lovers change their mind and make a dash for Gretna Green when he was not looking. He therefore was forced to remain with them throughout the long day. At night, after Lady Anne retired to her room, and Henry and Arthur retired to theirs, Arthur locked the door and removed the key.

"There is no need for that," said Henry. "I gave you my word that we will wait."

"Then there is no need to mind my taking possession of the key for the night, since you will not need it," said Arthur, slipping the key under his pillow.

Sir Charles arrived the next day, still pale but otherwise ready to play the role of stern father. However, when he saw that his stern looks made Lady Anne cry, he reverted to his usual kind self and assured the young lady that all would soon be well. When he learned Lady Carr was financing the venture, any thought of reprimand disappeared completely.

The Duke of Merton did not arrive until the sun was nearly setting. He was tired and hungry and in a terrible mood.

"Perhaps we should wait until the morning to tell him the news," Sir Charles said to Arthur.

Arthur begged to disagree. "This inn is too small for harboring secrets," he said. "If the Duke spies his daughter or Henry in a hallway or through a doorway, he will be furious we did not tell him."

However, Arthur did agree to at least wait until after the Duke had eaten the first course of his dinner and was feeling more refreshed. He took the news surprisingly well.

"To be honest, I have not the heroic spirit, nor the right constitution for the chase," he told Sir Charles and Arthur. "It is my stomach. I never could tolerate inn fare."

Sir Charles seized the opening that this topic provided and shared his own experience with the dubious fish. Soon the two gentlemen were chatting as amiably as if they were longtime friends, sharing stories about their various ailments, which they both agreed had been aggravated by the vicissitudes of the road. By dessert, they had moved on to a happier topic and had agreed upon terms for the marriage settlement. Paper and pen were called for, along with more wine, since this had been thirsty work, and received. After the marriage document was written and signed by the two parties, all that was left to do was finish off the cheese, which they did while finishing off the bottle of really good, old wine that the astute innkeeper had provided.

The journey back to London was uneventful, since Lady Anne was traveling in her father's carriage, while Henry was under the watchful eye of his father and elder brother. However, when they were resting for the night at an inn situated not too far from London, Arthur announced he would not be returning home with them.

"I have some business of my own to attend to," he said. The next morning he mounted the horse he had hired and rode away.

CHAPTER XIX

AFTER HENRY AND LADY ANNE departed, life at the cottage in Sevenoaks returned to its quiet routine. In the morning, if the weather was fine Sophie and Mrs. Hemingway would go for a long walk and gather leaves and herbs for Mrs. Hemingway's remedies. On one such morning, they ventured nearer than usual to the Harrington estate, Dunton Oaks, and Mrs. Hemingway asked Sophie if she would like to see the gardens or the great house.

"May we do so without an invitation?"

"I am acquainted with the housekeeper. Of course, we will not be able to see anything if Lord and Lady Harrington are at home, but I believe they are still in London."

The housekeeper greeted them cordially and thanked Mrs. Hemingway for some ointment she received the day before. Since that morning the cook had had an injury to her back while lifting a heavy pot, the housekeeper suggested Mrs. Hemingway go to the kitchen and give her advice, while she gave Sophie a tour of the house. They could meet in the gardens afterward.

"Only a few of the rooms are open to the public," said the housekeeper, "but there are some very fine paintings and furniture on display."

The first room they visited was a formal drawing room. The walls had been painted a dazzling deep yellow, a color motif that was echoed in the fabrics chosen for the furniture and the curtains, as well as the carpet. Large windows let in the morning sunlight, which was reflected back to them by the equally large mirrors set into the opposite wall. It was a much happier room than Sophie had expected to find, and she said as much to the housekeeper.

"This was the favorite room of the former Viscountess, the grandmother of the present Lord Harrington. Would you like to see her portrait?"

Sophie said that she would, and they returned to the corridor. The grand staircase was lined with the portraits of Lord and Lady Harringtons from the past, and the housekeeper pointed out the Lady Harrington who had inspired the yellow drawing room. A smiling, auburn-haired beauty stared back at Sophie from her gilt-framed perch.

"She was lovely," said Sophie.

The housekeeper sighed. "The house was a very different place, in her day."

"You knew her?"

"I was only a child, but I still remember the parties at Christmas. Each child who lived on the estate was invited to the yellow drawing room to receive a little gift from my lady's own hand. On Midsummer's Night there were pony rides and games on the great lawn. Those were happy times."

The housekeeper asked if Sophie would like to continue her tour, but Sophie had not yet had her fill of the portrait. She was particularly taken by the necklace that the beautiful woman was wearing.

"I have a necklace like that," said Sophie.

"I doubt it, Miss Moore. Those are the famous Harrington Rubies. Other than the Crown Jewels, I doubt there was a finer collection of rubies in all of England."

Sophie laughed at her mistake. "My necklace is only garnets, but it is a similar design." She then added, "I suppose the present Lady Harrington wears the necklace only on grand occasions."

"Unfortunately, the rubies disappeared."

"Were they stolen?"

"No one knows what happened to them. Fortunately, the incident happened after my lady had passed away. She would have been heartbroken — the necklace was a favorite of hers. Shall we continue?"

Sophie saw a few more rooms. Her knowledgeable guide pointed out the objects that were of real interest. Then the housekeeper suggested they find Mrs. Hemingway and continue on to the gardens.

"It seems a pity that no one lives here," Sophie commented. "All this grandeur, and no one to enjoy it."

"Perhaps once the present milord and milady have children they will spend more time here."

They found Mrs. Hemingway enjoying a coze in the kitchen with the cook, who was apparently feeling much better. However, Mrs. Hemingway promised to send over a fresh batch of her Sweet Chestnut ointment, just in case the pain should return.

When they were standing on the lawn, the housekeeper asked if they would like to see the woods, the stables or the Dower House.

"How is my lady feeling these days?" asked Mrs. Hemingway.

"I am afraid your ointments would be of no use for what ails her," replied the housekeeper. "But a visit might raise her spirits."

"Miss Moore is musical — perhaps she could play for my lady." Mrs. Hemingway then turned to Sophie and said, "You would not mind, would you, dear?"

Sophie assured the two women that she would be pleased to perform, but she also confessed her confusion. "I thought the former Lady Harrington passed away."

"That was the grandmother of the present Viscount. We are speaking about Lord Harrington's mother, the Dowager Viscountess," the housekeeper explained.

"I am sorry to hear she is not well," said Sophie.

"Perhaps I should prepare you for your visit," said the housekeeper. "Lady Harrington, the Dowager Viscountess, suffered a serious ailment after her husband died that has left her paralyzed on her left side. She is in a chair most of the time. It is also difficult for her to speak."

"Does no one come to visit her?" asked Mrs. Hemingway.

The housekeeper shook her head. "It is not for me to speak badly of my betters, but I do think it is a sad world we live in. It is as if she has died and is already in her grave, for all her former friends care."

By then they had reached the Dower House. Although it was not as large as the main house, it looked very grand, in Sophie's eyes. While a servant went to see if Lady Harrington wished to receive them, the housekeeper led the way to the music room. When she opened the door, Sophie nearly clapped her hands with delight.

The room was octagonal in shape, with long windows that reached from the ceiling to the floor and overlooked an expanse of lawn, bordered by a distant grove of evergreen trees. Sunlight was streaming into the room, endowing the elegant surroundings with an atmosphere of golden enchantment.

To Sophie's further delight, a harp was placed in the center of the room, and she instinctively moved toward it.

"Perhaps we should wait until my lady arrives," said Mrs. Hemingway.

While they waited, the housekeeper pointed out a few mechanical curios, all with a musical theme. Then they heard the sound of wheels approaching, and they turned toward the door.

A servant was pushing a chair fitted with wheels in both the front and the back. Sitting inside the chair was an elderly woman whose illness-ravaged face still showed glimpses of the beauty that she had possessed in happier times.

The housekeeper introduced the two visitors. The Dowager Viscountess signaled with her good hand toward the harp and Sophie took her seat before the instrument. She started with some light music, a cheerful country melody, and she thought she saw a look of approval in the ill woman's eye. Then she played a composition by Handel, which also seemed to be well received. However, that was the most the elder Lady Harrington could listen to that afternoon.

"My lady tires easily," the housekeeper explained, after the Dowager had been wheeled out of the room. "But would you be willing to return and play again, Miss Moore?"

Sophie assured the housekeeper that she would be delighted to play, whenever the Dowager wished.

As there was still a little time before the housekeeper needed to return to her duties, they finished the tour by walking to the stables, where Mr. Hemingway was busy helping the head groom, a man named Jenkins, train what looked like a rather high-spirited horse.

While Mr. Hemingway watched from the side, Jenkins attached a long rope to the horse's halter and with gentle but firm movements and words introduced the horse to its first commands: walk and halt. Although Mr. Hemingway did raise his hat to the ladies, it was clear his real interest was with the horse and Jenkins, and so the trio did not interrupt the work.

Sophie did, however, note that in just a very short time both Mr. and Mrs. Hemingway had succeeded in making themselves useful in their new home. She, on the other hand, had done nothing but water the garden with her tears. This sorry state of affairs strengthened her resolution to be of use to the Dowager Viscountness and provide that lady with at least a modicum of pleasure.

CHAPTER XX

SOPHIE BECAME ALMOST A DAILY visitor to the
Dower House. Although the elder Lady Harrington
found it uncomfortable to sit in her wheeled chair for
long stretches of time, she let it be known that Sophie
might play the harp whenever she liked. Sophie was
pleased to accept this gracious invitation, and she
could be found there most afternoons.

She had not entirely dismissed Henry and Lady
Anne from her mind. Therefore, when the post man
arrived with a letter for her, she eagerly broke the
seal and read its contents. It was only a quick note
from Henry. He once again thanked her and Mrs.
Hemingway for their assistance and informed them
that the final leg of the journey — across the border to
Scotland and Gretna Green — was not necessary after
all. The party was already on its way back to London,
where a conventional marriage ceremony would take
place within the month, to the happiness of both
families.

Mrs. Hemingway agreed that this was the best
ending to the episode, after Sophie shared the news.
She added that it was too bad the Duke of Merton did
not have an estate in the neighborhood; Henry
Wentworth's good spirits and engaging manners
would have added a welcome touch of gaiety to what
had become a rather dull place over the years.

Sophie agreed. But the letter, with its mention of
the Wentworth name, had brought with it other

thoughts and emotions. And she wondered whether the day would ever come when she could hear that name mentioned without feeling an ache in her heart.

LORD AND LADY HARRINGTON DID not spend much time at Sevenoaks—the county gentry were much too uncouth and uninteresting for Lady Harrington's taste—but they did entertain there on occasion. Thus, Arthur was not a stranger to either the place or the Dowager Viscountess. His plan therefore was to pay his respects to that lady and then ask to be allowed to wash the dust from his face and hands before joining her for tea. Then, his duty done to his hostess, the tea and his person, he intended to ride to the village to seek out Miss Moore.

The first part of his scheme seemed to be proceeding as he intended. The servant who answered the door took his riding cloak and gloves and hat, while a person from the stables took charge of his horse. Then he heard the music, and he hoped Lady Harrington had not decided to have a concert in her home that afternoon. If so, he would not be able to escape for several hours and he was too agitated to listen to music while his future happiness still hung in the balance.

When he approached the music room, the sun was shining so brightly that at first he saw only the harp, but not the player. When he did realize who the player was, his heart skipped a beat. The vision she presented, surrounded as she was by beams of golden light that seemed to dance about the harp and suffuse the room with magic, took his breath away.

The song came to an end, and Sophie set the harp back into its standing position. She glanced over at the Dowager Viscountess, who was dozing in her chair, as that lady often did, and then Sophie rose from her seat.

When her gaze drifted over to the doorway — and she saw him standing there — her hand instinctively went to her throat, where a cry was beginning to form. So many days had passed since Lady Harrington's visit — that awful day when Sophie had been forced to give up her one hope for happiness forever — that Sophie had begun to believe that perhaps Arthur Wentworth had never meant to propose to her; or that perhaps he had changed his mind.

When she had considered the possibility that he might come to her, she had assumed he would send a message first, to prepare her for his visit. They would meet in the front room of the cottage or the garden — a place where she felt at her ease and in control. It had never occurred to her that they might meet here and all of sudden, when she was totally unprepared.

Arthur, too, hesitated. Although he had had ample time to rehearse this scene during the long journey to and from Scotland, now that the moment had arrived he found himself utterly without words.

Yet, he was a man, and a man's instincts are to move forward. He therefore crossed the room and took Sophie's hand and raised it to his lips.

"Miss Moore, I know this must seem to you sudden, too sudden. But, I love you, Miss Moore. I love you more than anything else in the world. Would you do me the honor of marrying me?"

Sophie was silent. Inside her a battle was raging. With all her heart and soul, she wanted to say yes, to shout the word. But she could not forget the promise she had made in a moment of thoughtlessness, when she had signed her name to the statement of debt that she owed to Lady Harrington.

She removed her hand from his and turned away. "I am sorry. I thank you, Mr. Wentworth, for the honor you have bestowed upon me. But I cannot marry you."

"Forgive me. I should not have spoken so hastily. It is natural that you wish some time to think, to ..."

She shook her head and tried to silence his words with her hand, which he once again grasped in his.

"Will you not at least give me reason to hope that after you have had time to reflect you might change your mind?"

Arthur, of course, expected to receive an affirmative answer. A woman might refuse a first offer for many reasons, but it almost never signified a real refusal. However, he was surprised to see that Miss Moore had turned very pale, when the situation called for maidenly blushes on her cheeks.

"I will not change my mind, Mr. Wentworth. Never."

"Never is a very strong word, Miss Moore."

"I know," said Sophie, turning back to him, so that she was looking into his eyes. "That is why I chose it. Goodbye, Mr. Wentworth."

Sophie rushed out of the room. Arthur watched her go. This, he had not expected, and he had no idea how to proceed.

ALTHOUGH THE CRISIS WAS OVER, Sophie felt far from relieved. She could not even confide all that was in her heart to Mrs. Hemingway. That good woman had taught Sophie that a person always felt better after doing the right thing. Sophie had done the right thing, she had kept her word, she had repaid her debt of honor, but she was miserable.

Mrs. Hemingway could not help but see the change in her young charge. Time, that great healer, seemed to have lost its power. Instead of becoming gradually more cheerful and at peace, Sophie seemed more depressed and agitated than ever.

"Something has happened," she said the next morning, when she and Sophie were taking their walk.

"I ... I am only concerned about my future."

"It is true there are few opportunities for you here in Sevenoaks, but when my sister returns I will speak to her. Her husband's family lives in Manchester and they may know people. The nobility are not the only ones who like music. There are merchants and manufacturers up north who can afford to pay for musical instruction for their daughters and ... Why, Sophie, you are crying. You can tell me, child. Surely, by now I have proven myself to be worthy of your confidences."

"It is nothing, really," Sophie replied, trying to laugh away her tears. "It is just that yesterday Mr. Wentworth proposed to me, while I was at Lady Harrington's. I refused him, of course."

Sophie continued to walk. Indeed, she fairly ran forward. She felt she must keep moving or she would collapse. Mrs. Hemingway, however, had stopped in her tracks.

"Sophie, come back here! At once!"

Sophie recognized the tone of voice. It was the one Mrs. Hemingway had used when Sophie was a child and had done something wrong and tried to hide that fact from adult eyes. Despite the reprimand that voice conveyed, it was also comforting because it was familiar. Sophie therefore returned to where Mrs. Hemingway was standing.

"I thought you said you were in love with Mr. Wentworth."

"I am."

"Then why did you refuse him."

"Because I ... I gave my word to someone that I would not marry him."

"To that aunt of his?"

Sophie shook her head.

"Then to who?"

"To Lady Harrington, the present Viscountness."

"Why on earth did you do that?"

Sophie had no choice but to tell over the entire story, which she did as briefly as she could.

Mrs. Hemingway was astounded. She, too, could see no way out of the conundrum. "I must talk this over with Mr. Hemingway," was the best she could say.

ASTOUNDED WAS AN ACCURATE DESCRIPTION for Arthur, as well. There had been a note of finality in Sophie's rejection that he could not ignore. Much as he tried to find some other way to interpret her words, as well as the look she had given him before she left the music room, he could find no other meaning. She did not love him.

Being a man, he did not go home and sulk in his room. That was what a gentlemen's club was for. He therefore became practically a permanent fixture at White's, drinking too much, betting too heavily, doing all the things a gentleman did when he was in a brown study. Fortunately, the rest of the family was too busy with preparations for the upcoming marriage of Henry and Lady Anne to pay him much notice.

He had even avoided the company of his cousin, but Lady Harrington found an opportunity to seek him out. Sir Charles and the Duke of Merton could not decide on where the young married couple should live in London. There were two properties under consideration. Each possessed a good address and spacious rooms. In short, to a gentleman's eye they seemed almost alike. It took a woman with experience running a household to determine which would be most comfortable, and although Miss Dorothea Wentworth had that experience Sir Charles would never consult her about anything truly important. The new Duchess of Merton was too busy with acquiring a new wardrobe befitting her new station of life to spare a few hours away from the dressmaker. Sir Charles therefore begged Lady Harrington to assist them, and she graciously accepted.

She arrived at the Wentworth home wearing a striking primrose-colored walking costume. It was topped by a turban of the same color that was trimmed with ermine. She carried a large ermine muff, instead of a parasol, since the weather had once again turned dreary and cold.

Sir Charles regarded her with approval. "As always, Mary, you bring sunshine with you wherever you go."

Lady Harrington accepted the compliment, and then asked who would be accompanying them on their tour of the two residences. When Sir Charles replied that their party would be a small one — only Henry would be joining them — she inquired after Arthur.

"I hope he is in good health. One sees him so infrequently these days."

"I believe he is in the billiards room now, if you wish to see him." Sir Charles then added, "Something is wrong there, Mary. It might only be the fact that Henry will be marrying before him — brotherly rivalry and all that. I do not know. But if you could discover what is bothering Arthur, and find a way to cheer him up, I would be in your debt."

"I will do what I can," she said, bestowing her brightest smile upon Sir Charles.

Since Mary was like a daughter, as Sir Charles so often said, she had free run of the house. Therefore, even though Miss Dorothea Wentworth never went into the billiards room, which was an exclusively male domain according to the rules of the Wentworth home, Lady Harrington felt no such qualms. She entered and shut the door behind her, so she could speak to Arthur quite in private.

"If I did not know you so well, Arthur, I would think you were avoiding me."

Arthur kept his eye on his game. "Perhaps I am."

"Do not tell me. You have been to Sevenoaks."

Arthur applied white chalk to the tip of his cue. "Suppose I have."

"Will you tell me what happened, or must I guess?"

"I do not see why it concerns you."

"A love scene always interests a lady."

Arthur ignored her as he walked to the other side of the table. He made his shot. The red ball went hurtling across the baize covering and into the side pocket.

"Very well, if you will not tell, I shall guess. You got down on your knees before the woman you adore — and she refused you. Well, am I right? At least partially?"

"Obviously, the lady refused me. You would have heard of my marriage plans, if she had accepted."

Arthur retrieved the red ball and prepared for another shot.

"And now your pride is hurt. One small rejection and you crumple. How like a man!"

"You seem to forget that I am in love with Miss Moore. It is hardly a small matter to me."

"And you seem to forget who you are talking to, Arthur." Lady Harrington reached across the billiards table and grabbed the other end of the wooden cue. "You are in love with me. You always were, and you always will be. That is why I could not let Miss Moore come between us."

"What on earth are you talking about?"

Lady Harrington released the cue and playfully nudged one of the white balls forward and into a nearby pocket with her gloved finger. "I went to Sevenoaks the day you and your father went running after Henry and Lady Anne."

"Why did you do that?"

"Several weeks ago, Miss Moore foolishly signed her name to a little document I had written, in which she affirmed that she owed me a favor. I decided the time had come for her to pay her debt. Do you know what I asked for, Arthur? I demanded you. I demanded that she give you up."

"You have worked everything out, haven't you?"

"Yes, I have. You may marry Miss Bryce-Jones or Lady Jane, whichever one you choose. It matters as little to me as I am sure it matters to you. After the wedding, you will play the faithful, devoted husband for a few months or so, at least until the bridal trip is over. And then we can be together, whenever we choose. No one will talk. No one will care. We will be just two boring married people, doing what two boring married people do."

"In our circle?"

"What other circle matters?"

"Have you not forgotten something, Mary?"

"Have I?"

"If words spoken at the altar do not matter, why should Miss Moore take seriously her promise to you?"

"Ah, because she is not in our circle. Little fools like Miss Moore take a debt of honor seriously. When they give their word they mean it."

They heard Sir Charles call Lady Harrington's name. She gathered up her muff and gave Arthur her hand. When he did not take it, she said, "Mope. Pine. Gnash your teeth in anger. But you will come back to me. And when you do, Arthur, I promise I will make you forget all about your little Miss Moore."

CHAPTER XXI

KNOWING THE TRUTH BEHIND MISS Moore's refusal did nothing to ease Arthur's depressed spirits. If anything, it made things worse. He loved her even more intensely for being that increasingly rare creature, a woman of honor and courage, and he was in agony that he could not possess her without destroying the very things about her that he so admired.

As for Lady Harrington, he could not see his cousin without wishing her in Jericho, even though that did nothing to rectify the harm she had done.

He still kept busy, filling his days and nights with meaningless amusements. When Henry therefore asked him to come to Tattersall's, to choose a team of horses for the new carriage that Lady Anne must have, since she was a Duke's daughter and the Duke of Merton had ordered a grand carriage for his only child, Arthur accepted the invitation.

As a nonpareil, Arthur was expected to know everything there was to know about horses, and he prided himself that he did. He and Henry leisurely walked through the covered galleries, observing the animals on display. However, as they walked, Arthur had the curious sensation that he was being observed, as well. He then realized the familiar figure observing him was the head groom at the Harrington estate in Sevenoaks, a man named Jenkins.

Since Tattersall's was the sort of place where horseflesh was the main topic, it was not strange for a gentleman to converse with a groom. Arthur and Henry therefore greeted Jenkins, who in turn introduced his companion, Mr. Hemingway. Once the Sevenoaks acquaintanceship was recalled, Henry greeted Mr. Hemingway like an old friend. Arthur also observed Mr. Hemingway with interest, after learning of his connection with Miss Moore.

The four compared notes about the horses on display and agreed that this day, at least, there were none worth bidding for.

"It is a shame," said Jenkins. "One of the horses belonging to Lady Harrington has gone lame, and we have come all the way from Kent."

Arthur took the hint and invited the two visitors from Kent to partake of some refreshments. Jenkins was happy to converse about horseflesh while he sipped his ale. Mr. Hemingway was equally happy not to speak, and to observe Mr. Arthur Wentworth at close quarters.

When there was a lull in the conversation, Arthur asked, "How do you find England, Mr. Hemingway? I understand you were away for many years."

"In truth, sir, Jamaica weather suits me better. I have lost my taste for the rain and cold. But my wife wished to return to her home — she grew up in Sevenoaks — and, well, you know what a wife is."

"I am afraid I have not had that honor."

Jenkins took the opportunity to congratulate Henry on his upcoming marriage, while Arthur tried to think of a way to turn the topic to Miss Moore. But he could not, and the moment passed. Henry and Jenkins began to enthusiastically discuss the merits of the Yorkshire Trotter versus the Norfolk Trotter, and which would be a better horse for a London carriage. By the time the pair decided it was impossible to decide, it was time for Jenkins and Mr. Hemingway to begin the return trip home to Kent.

"WELL, I HAVE SEEN HIM."

Sophie had gone up to bed, and so it was only Mr. and Mrs. Hemingway sitting in the front room.

While Mr. Hemingway had been smoking his pipe, Mrs. Hemingway had been doing some mending. She now put down her needle and said, "You have seen who?"

"Arthur Wentworth. He was at Tattersall's. With his brother Henry."

"And pray, sir, what is your opinion of him?"

"He knows about horses."

Mrs. Hemingway knew her husband could not bestow a higher compliment upon a man. However, she also knew that knowledge about horseflesh was one thing, while possessing the qualities necessary to be a good husband were another.

"He did not say anything about Sophie, I suppose?"

Mr. Hemingway thought for a moment. "In a matter of speaking he did." He then repeated the conversation they had. "He has not made an offer to another young lady."

Mrs. Hemingway was not convinced this showed great constancy on the young man's part, since not that much time had passed, and she said so. "Did you observe nothing more?"

Mr. Hemingway again took his time before answering. "He has a good eye."

This caught Mrs. Hemingway's attention. Her husband often spoke about a horse's eye, how an experienced trainer could tell a horse's disposition from the look in its eye; whether or not the horse would prove to be malleable and good-natured, nervous and easily excited or frightened, or shifty and always ready to bolt.

"He has a good-natured eye? Is that what you mean to say?"

Mr. Hemingway shook his head. Like most experienced horse trainers, he worked more with touch than words, which in his opinion were poor vessels for holding any real depth of meaning. He could never understand why women had an incomprehensible need to cram a perfectly good thought, boundless in its possibilities, into limited speech, but he did understand that he would have no peace until he satisfied Mrs. Hemingway with a more complete explanation.

"Mr. Henry Wentworth has a good-natured eye. The brother has something more."

"Something more in a good way?" Mrs. Hemingway, for her part, knew there was no point in rushing her husband. He would come to the point, eventually, in his usual roundabout way.

"Something more in a Miss Moore sort of way." Mr. Hemingway chuckled over his little jest.

"You mean you feel they are similar, well-matched?"

"I could see them as a team."

Mrs. Hemingway gave her husband a knowing look. "Then we must act."

Mr. Hemingway was not sure. "You would have to tell. You always said it was better not to."

"That was before, when the news could bring Sophie no real good — but possibly a great deal of harm. Now, everything has changed."

IT WAS A PITY THE Dowager Viscountess was so ill, for if she had not been it would have saved Mrs. Hemingway much trouble. She could have asked the elder Lady Harrington to invite the concerned persons to Sevenoaks, instead of having to arrange a gathering in London. But when the happiness of her young charge was at stake — and she still thought of Sophie as her young charge — Mrs. Hemingway must think nothing of the inconvenience of traveling to London by coach. She also thought nothing of bringing Mr. Hemingway in tow, since she and Sophie must have a chaperon for their journey.

"You have brought the garnet necklace, Sophie?" she asked for perhaps the dozenth time.

Sophie replied in the affirmative, although she could not see what importance the necklace could have on the outcome of their journey. Indeed, Mrs. Hemingway had been so secretive that Sophie scarcely knew the reason for their hasty departure to London. That it was not to be a permanent move was made clear by the fact that they had left their trunks and belongings in Sevenoaks. Yet, knowing that none of them had any relations in London or business concerns that needed their immediate attention, she was at a loss to explain their journey.

However, her fears began to grow when the coach reached London and traveled on to Mayfair. As they passed streets and sights that Sophie only too vividly recalled, her alarm grew. And when the coach stopped before the home belonging to Sir Charles Wentworth, she shrank into her corner, determined that not even wild horses would succeed in dragging her from the safety of the carriage.

A servant came out to open the carriage door and let down the steps. Mrs. Hemingway allowed herself to be handed out of the coach. Mr. Hemingway followed. Sophie did not.

"I do not understand," she protested.

"You will," said Mrs. Hemingway, in a voice that brooked no dissent.

Sophie reluctantly allowed herself to be helped out of the carriage. She followed Mr. and Mrs. Hemingway up the front steps and through the open door. However, it was only due to a strong yank on her arm that she was propelled through the door that led into the drawing room.

Sir Charles rose to welcome the newcomers. But even though he strove to play his usual part of congenial host, his words were more constrained than usual. His eye fell upon Mr. and Mrs. Hemingway, whose dress and demeanor showed to all the world that they were not the usual sort to be entertained in the Wentworth drawing room, and Sir Charles hesitated while he decided whether they could remain standing or should be shown to some empty seats.

His greeting to Sophie was also more restrained, and she felt sorry for his discomfort almost more than her own. She longed to tell him that her presence there was not her choice; if she had known this was the destination, she would not have come.

Henry, as always, came to her rescue and showed Sophie to a seat. While Mr. and Mrs. Hemingway were also seated, Sophie kept her head down. She assumed Arthur Wentworth was somewhere in the room, but she was too embarrassed to look.

There was an awkward silence for a few moments, and then Lady Carr, taking charge of the situation as always, said, "You have something to say, Mrs. Hemingway?"

"Indeed, I do," replied that woman, who had no qualms about meeting the eye of anyone in the room, including Lady Carr. "Sir Charles, I do not expect you to remember me, or that before I was married to Mr. Hemingway in Jamaica my name was Harriet Jones and I served as a lady's maid in the former Lord Harrington's estate at Sevenoaks."

"No, I cannot say I do, Mrs. Jones, er, Hemingway."

"Well, it was and I did. But perhaps you will recall the young lady who was my mistress, Miss Catherine Harrington."

"Miss Catherine ..." The eyes of Sir Charles lit up with the memory of that woman. "Of course, I remember Miss Harrington. She was a great friend of my wife."

"Indeed, she was. And perhaps, Sir Charles, you recall what became of Miss Harrington, my mistress?"

Sir Charles glanced over to the other side of the room. Sophie followed his glance, but it had fallen upon a gentleman she did not know. However, since he was seated next to Lady Harrington, she assumed this must be Lord Harrington, the current Viscount.

Although Lord Harrington was looking very bored and oblivious, Sir Charles still hesitated.

"Really, Mrs. Hemingway," he said at last, "there are ladies present. I do not think it would be quite the thing ..."

"Don't be an idiot," said Lady Carr, her eyes gleaming with anticipation of hearing a good story. "Go on, Mrs. Hemingway, tell us what became of her."

"Miss Harrington fell in love with a young soldier, who was on leave from his regiment stationed in Jamaica. They eloped to Gretna Green, where they were married. And if you ask how I know the marriage took place, I was the abigail who accompanied Miss Harrington to Scotland. I saw them exchange vows with my own eyes."

Mrs. Hemingway cast a defiant look about the room, daring anyone to doubt her word. No one did.

"My mistress had hoped her father would forgive her and welcome her young husband into the family, but the former Viscount refused to acknowledge her. He cut her off without a penny, or even one kind word."

"So it was young Moore that Miss Harrington ran off with," said Sir Charles, still trying to assimilate this news. "My wife was heartbroken when she found out Miss Harrington had been disinherited and thrown out of her home. No one knew exactly what had happened, since the family hushed it up. And when we never heard from Miss Harrington again, well, naturally we feared the worst."

"But what happened to the young couple?" asked Henry, who had become interested in the story, after the mention of Gretna Green.

"They went to Jamaica, and the young soldier rejoined his regiment. Miss Harrington begged me to come with them. I believe she was very afraid to travel so far from home."

"Yes, I can believe that she would be," said Henry, recalling the bravery Lady Anne had shown while on their journey, as well as those moments when the young lady had expressed some fear, as was only natural.

"I think some of you here can guess the rest of my story," said Mrs. Hemingway. Once again she cast a defiant glance about the room, as though daring anyone to try and stop her from continuing with her tale. For the moment, though, she had the group's attention and so she could carry on unimpeded.

"A year later, my mistress gave birth to a little girl, but she did not live to hold her darling child in her arms more than a few minutes. The last words of my mistress, Mrs. Catherine Moore, were to me, when she asked me to look after her little girl, Sophie."

Sophie, who had been following the story closely, had guessed where the story was leading, but she still gave a little gasp when she heard her name mentioned. No one had ever told her the full story of her mother's history, or how her parents had met.

"A very touching story, Mrs. Hemingway, but how do we know it is true?" asked Lady Harrington, raising an eyebrow to show that she, at least, was not convinced.

Mrs. Hemingway turned to Sophie and said, "Sophie, the necklace."

Sophie opened her reticule and removed a leather pouch. Her fingers trembled slightly as she loosened the strings that held it shut. She still could not understand what role the necklace had to play in these proceedings, but she removed from the pouch her first and last present from her mother.

"Here it is, Mrs. Hemingway," she said reaching out her hand, while the gems dangled from her fingers, catching the light. "Here is my garnet necklace."

"Not garnets, Sophie," replied Mrs. Hemingway. "Rubies."

"The Harrington Rubies!" exclaimed Lord Harrington, fully awake for the first time. "Where did you get those? How ..."

He made a lunge forward to snatch them from Sophie's hand, but Arthur had also stepped forward and blocked him.

"If we let Mrs. Hemingway finish her story, perhaps this too will become clear," said Arthur, as he led Lord Harrington back to his seat.

"I do not see why we must listen to any more of this ... fairy tale," said Miss Dorothea Wentworth. "It is obvious to me that this old woman is a colossal liar. She and her husband, if he really is her husband, probably stole the necklace and escaped to Jamaica. And I would not be surprised if Miss Moore was really their daughter and not the daughter of Miss Harrington."

"Well said," said Lady Harrington, giving Miss Wentworth an approving look.

Mrs. Hemingway had come prepared for this accusation. She withdrew a letter from her reticule. "I ask no one to accept my word. But the word of the Dowager Viscountess, Lady Harrington, that I believe is different."

"Well, of course," said Sir Charles, looking very uncomfortable. As a baronet, he had a natural respect for the British aristocracy — as well as a fear of incurring the wrath of those who were higher up on the social ladder and had the ability to blackball people like him from the best clubs and dinner parties. "No one here would wish to insult Lord Harrington's mother."

"Then you may all read this letter from Lady Harrington at your leisure. I asked her to set down in writing her account of what happened all those years ago. She freely admits that she gave Miss Catherine Harrington the ruby necklace of her own free will, so the young lady would not be totally penniless."

"Penniless?" said Lord Harrington. "That necklace is worth a fortune. If my father had known what my mother had done ..."

"Precisely," said Mrs. Hemingway. "That is why her ladyship never told anyone. She let your father believe the necklace had been stolen. Perhaps you, Lord Harrington, would like to read the letter first and verify that this is your mother's handwriting."

Lord Harrington eagerly snatched up the letter. The handwriting of the elderly Lady Harrington was not easy to read, since her infirmity made it difficult for her to hold a pen. But the son affirmed that the letter had, indeed, been written by his mother. He also declared that his mother confirmed all the details of Mrs. Hemingway's tale.

"Then you acknowledge that Miss Sophie Moore is your cousin, the daughter of your aunt, Catherine Harrington, and the granddaughter of your grandfather, the Viscount Harrington?"

Lord Harrington hesitated, as he tried to sort out the details of what this acknowledgment might cost him. The entailed lands caused him no problem. A female cousin could have no claim to them. But there were other properties, and even if he seldom visited them he had no desire to give them up. His slow-witted brain finally worked itself around to what he felt was the correct, compromise solution. "Only in a manner of speaking — place on the family tree, that sort of thing. But since my aunt was disinherited, Miss Moore is not really part of the family, at least not in the legal sense of the word," he said, very pleased, for a moment.

"Sophie, put away your necklace," commanded Mrs. Hemingway.

"But ... but ..." Lord Harrington looked about the room for assistance.

"If you say Miss Moore is not a Harrington, my lord," said Mrs. Hemingway, "then these rubies are not Harringtons either."

Lord Harrington cut a somewhat ridiculous figure as he vacillated between greed and family pride, his gaze moving back and forth between Sophie and the rubies. Finally, greed won the day. "Miss Moore, cousin, ma'am," he stammered. "Pleased to meet you, I am sure."

Lady Harrington made a movement to leave, but Mrs. Hemingway was not yet finished.

"I believe, Lady Harrington, that you extracted a promise from Miss Moore, as payment for a certain debt of honor."

Sophie sprang from her seat and rushed over to Mrs. Hemingway. "No, please, not in front of all these people," she frantically whispered.

"Courage, Sophie. Never retreat when the enemy is on the run."

Mrs. Hemingway then looked straight ahead, as though she were addressing a jury of her peers. "It is the opinion of Mr. Hemingway, and myself that the document in question, commonly known as vowels, is no longer valid. That document was signed by Miss Sophie Moore, the orphaned daughter of a poor soldier and his wife — a nobody who was the daughter of nobodies. But no such person exists. The true Miss Moore is a granddaughter of a peer of the realm, and that person never gave her vowels to anyone, including Lady Harrington."

CHAPTER XXII

THOUGH IT IS TRUE THAT Mrs. Hemingway's argument might not have held up in a real court of law, it was almost unanimously accepted in the court of public opinion that was in session in the Wentworth drawing room that day.

While Sir Charles congratulated Lord Harrington on the return of the missing jewels, and while Henry congratulated Mr. and Mrs. Hemingway on their excellent argument and the way they had carried the day, and while Lady Carr invited Henry and the Hemingways to a game of whist as a token of appreciation for such an agreeable story, and while Lady Harrington and Miss Wentworth exchanged sour comments and looks, Arthur whisked Sophie away to the library, where they could speak undisturbed.

In truth, they did not say so much. At least that is what little William said, when he reported back to the kitchen, where the servants were having their tea. William had been sent to the library to sweep around the fireplace, totally unaware of the great events that were about to overtake him. He was, indeed, busy at work when Mr. Wentworth and Miss Moore entered the room. At once, he sized up the situation. If he were to leave the room with his work unfinished, he would get a scolding from the butler — and cook might refuse to give him a slice of her excellent plum cake. Such a dire consequence most be avoided at all costs. He therefore decided to quietly wait behind the large screen that shielded the fireplace from the rest of the room, and luckily was large enough to shield him from view and see how events would develop.

"It was like this," said William, when he was in the kitchen, enjoying his newfound importance with the household staff. "Mr. Arthur, he says, 'Miss Moore.' Just like that. 'Miss Moore.'"

William took a bite of bread and butter. The cook grew impatient. "Well, go on, my boy. What happened next?"

William finished chewing. "Miss Sophie, she just stood there looking all dreamy-eyed."

"If yer was behind the screen, how do yer know?" asked a young stable hand, who was more than a little put out by William's rapid rise to prominence in the household.

"I know, because I peeked around the screen to see if maybe they had gone, so I could get on with my work."

William, who had dreams of bettering himself, glanced at the butler, who gave him a nod of approval.

"Miss Moore didn't say anything?" asked the cook, impatient to hear the whole story before her soup burnt.

"Certainly she said something. She said, 'Yes, Mr. Wentworth?'"

One of the young footmen rolled his eyes. "If that ain't the gentry for you. It's a wonder any of them manage to get shackled."

"Sssh, let William talk," said the cook. "Go on, William. Who spoke next, Mr. Arthur or Miss Sophie?"

"It was Mr. Arthur, as I recall. But he didn't say much. Just, 'Will you?' And then Miss Sophie, she just said again, 'Yes, Mr. Wentworth.'"

"Did they kiss?" asked the under-parlor maid.

William gave the presumptuous girl a look of disdain, before helping himself to a second slice of bread and butter.

"A gentleman never tells."

If you enjoyed Jericho's Child, *please consider leaving a review at your favorite online booksellers.*

*Enjoy These Other Books
By Jolie Beaumont:*

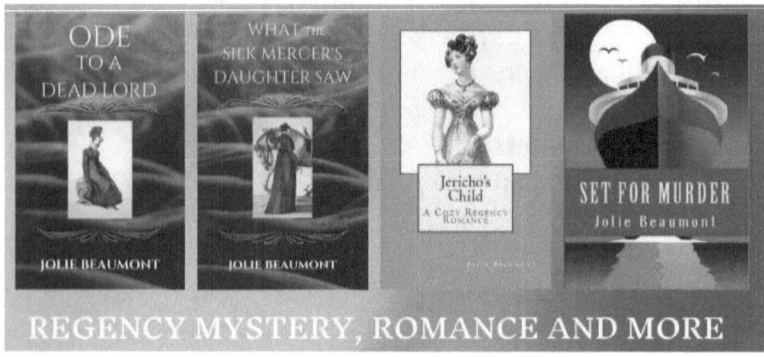

Ode to a Dead Lord
A Theo Bryght, Runner Mystery
"A brilliant story about murder, deception and love" —
Regency Inkwell

It is the summer of 1812. Wellington is fighting Napoleon's army in Spain, Lord Byron is dazzling the Beau Monde with the first Canto of his *Childe Harold's Pilgrimage* – and Viscount Percy Ainsford Foster Ashe is discovered dead in a shabby boarding house in Brighton.

Who would want to murder Viscount Ashe? Is there more to his gambling addiction than meets the eye? Is there any chance that the now penniless widow, Lady Charlotte Ashe, will ever recover her lost fortune? These questions haunt Lady Ashe after she returns to her home in the North York Moors — for as she and Bow Street Runner Theo Bryght soon find out, her husband's death may be just the first canto in a deadly ode to revenge.

What the Silk Mercer's Daughter Saw
A Theo Bryght, Runner Mystery
"A good clean mystery" - Amazon.com

In this new Regency mystery featuring Bow Street Runner Theo Bryght, he encounters not only dark passions and devastating secrets, but also a second chance to win the love of his life, Lady Charlotte Ashe.

Set for Murder
A Showbiz Is Murder Mystery
"Charming and suspenseful" – Amazon.com

It's the height of the Depression, but for Penny and Nick Garnett, two young Broadway stars about to make their London debut, life feels like one long musical comedy show — until a duchess is found murdered in her cabin. Who would want to murder the young and beautiful duchess? That's the question Scotland Yard Inspector Guy Travers must solve. When he begins to suspect an over-the-hill vaudeville performer, Penny and Nick rush to help their thespian friend. But with the ship now turned into a "set for murder," will they solve the mystery before the murderer comes back for a second act?

For information about future books by Jolie Beaumont, visit her website at
joliebeaumont.weebly.com